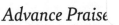

"Surfaces deceive. LeBlanc's deliciously creepy stories revel in pushing past the limitations of the body, of the domestic, and of the known even when this means guts are going to spill. In the tradition of writers such as Shirley Jackson, Daphne du Maurier, and Lisa Tuttle, these stories disorient and slide from the familiar and dreamy and into the nightmarish in the most thrilling of ways. LeBlanc kidnaps the reader and takes them on an unforgettable, screamingly great ride."—SUZETTE MAYR, AUTHOR OF *THE SLEEPING CAR PORTER*, WINNER OF THE GILLER PRIZE)

"Amy LeBlanc's *Homebodies* is like a slow, sliding kaleidoscope of dreams. A series of glimpses into strained, disjointed families and communities, the book follows a network of disquieting characters with wounds—both figurative and very literal—that fester and pulse. The stories feel like admissions, like muffled secrets passed behind closed doors. They are fragmented but nonetheless full—dense and swollen with the characters' blunted fears, their stark needs. LeBlanc's writing is a shudder running through the body: a sensation that is visceral, reflexive, and inescapable. Like a boa snake constricting, like peristalsis, these stories will swallow you whole."—ERICA MCKEEN, AUTHOR OF *TEAR*

"Amy LeBlanc's uncanny, open-ended stories perfectly capture the ambiguous anxieties of our pandemic times. This is an engrossing, contemporary, well-arranged collection with novelistic immersiveness." —SEYWARD GOODHAND, AUTHOR OF *EVEN THAT WILDEST HOPE*

"In *Homebodies*, Amy LeBlanc moves time forward and backward, and mostly—underneath—families, lovers, cats and friends. In these stories, growing up doesn't lighten the dark, understanding doesn't sweeten the lot, sadness and despair compete with spirit for space. It's LeBlanc who makes darkness palatable with her poignancy and poetic touch. Don't plan on putting *Homebodies* down after you pick it up."—SUSIE MOLONEY, AUTHOR OF *THE DWELLING* AND *THE THIRTEEN*

Homebodies

STORIES

Amy LeBlanc

Enfield & Wizenty (an imprint of Great Plains Publications)
320 Rosedale Ave
Winnipeg, MB R3L 1L8
www.greatplains.mb.ca

Great Plains Publications gratefully acknowledges the financial support provided for its publishing program by the Government of Canada through the Canada Book Fund; the Canada Council for the Arts; the Province of Manitoba through the Book Publishing Tax Credit and the Book Publisher Marketing Assistance Program; and the Manitoba Arts Council.

Design & Typography by Relish New Brand Experience
Printed in Canada by Friesens

Library and Archives Canada Cataloguing in Publication

Title: Homebodies : stories / by Amy Leblanc.
Names: LeBlanc, Amy, 1995- author.
Identifiers: Canadiana (print) 20220491372 | Canadiana (ebook) 20220491380 |
     ISBN 9781773371016 (softcover) | ISBN 9781773371023 (ebook)
Subjects: LCGFT: Short stories.
Classification: LCC PS8623.E323 H66 2023 | DDC c813/.6—dc23

ENVIRONMENTAL BENEFITS STATEMENT

Great Plains Publications saved the following resources by printing the pages of this book on chlorine free paper made with 100% post-consumer waste.

TREES	WATER	ENERGY	SOLID WASTE	GREENHOUSE GASES
4	360	2	15	1,940
FULLY GROWN	GALLONS	MILLION BTUs	POUNDS	POUNDS

Environmental impact estimates were made using the Environmental Paper Network Paper Calculator 4.0. For more information visit www.papercalculator.org

Canada

FSC
www.fsc.org
MIX
Paper from responsible sources
FSC® C016245

"Slack your rope, Hangsaman,
O slack it for a while,
I think I see my true love coming,
Coming many a mile"
SHIRLEY JACKSON, *HANGSAMAN*

"One need not be a chamber—
to be haunted—"
EMILY DICKINSON

Table of Contents

The Fox
(in the House)

Twisted

The day I lost Camilla was the same day that Andy MacArthur was sentenced to life in prison. I didn't hear about the outcome of the trial until I'd returned home. I had searched for two hours and fifty-five minutes. At two hours and fifty-six minutes, I caved and phoned Sam and then the police. Once Sam understood what I was saying, she berated me for not having called the police first. By the end of the day, my frostbitten fingertips were thawing in a mixing bowl filled with warm water. I knew that I would never see Camilla again and that Sam wouldn't speak to me. Sam was my only friend with a child.

As my fingers defrosted, I picked up my phone to search for articles about the trial. Andy had pleaded not guilty. The mother of one of his victims, the eighth, fainted during the trial and had to be carried from the courtroom. Andy's parents were not present. I had only known Andy peripherally; we had seven mutual friends on Facebook, and then none in the scramble to sever all ties and any digital trail of acquaintance. At parties, he stood in the corner behind the chips and dip; he read books in coffee shops; he didn't talk to strangers on the train; he wore white running shoes. And then, one day, I saw his face on the news. For once, he hadn't relegated himself to the corner—his face covered the entire screen and then disappeared and was replaced by photos of the fourteen individuals he had murdered, dismembered, and interred on his parents' acreage outside of Calgary. He had kept his victims in a deep freezer until spring when the ground had thawed enough to dig. He looked more pointed, more drawn out and angular in the photo they used than he ever had in real life. I hadn't noticed that his hair was the colour of rusted nails. It occurred to me later that I had only ever seen him wearing a hat.

I should have felt shocked or disgusted at having known him or having been at parties where I was in proximity to him, but he was peripheral enough that I could call him a stranger. Once I deleted him from Facebook, he became one.

For Christmas, I had gifted Camilla with a Mary-Kate and Ashley hair twister I picked up at Value Village. Only a few strands remained from the previous owner, but I plucked them out with tweezers and it was good as new. It coiled two strands of her hair together which she could fasten with a bead at the ends. That winter morning, she had twined so many strands that the beads at the ends of her braids clanked against one another when she went up and down on the opposite end of the seesaw. Her jacket was a shade of yellow that reminded me of highlighters I'd bought in university but had never actually used. It was mid-winter and the temperature hadn't lifted above minus thirty in three weeks. Camilla insisted we go to the playground even though it felt tantamount to suicide.

I could picture Camilla after Sam tucked her into bed. I used to be the one who tucked her in and slept over when Sam needed to travel for work. Camilla would refuse to take out her braids even though they gave her a headache and she would fall asleep with her lips slightly parted as if she was always on the verge of speaking.

Sam thought I was distracted by the trial. She said she hadn't been able to get any work done in weeks because she couldn't stop seeing the faces of his victims every time she closed her eyes. She had enabled news alerts for Andy's name and the names of his victims so that she would be informed of any developments as quickly as possible. Sam thought that if she was obsessed, I must have been too.

Months before the day at the playground and Andy's sentencing, Sam had sat in my living room sipping at a steaming cup of decaf coffee. Camilla kept herself occupied by making faces at the entryway mirror.

"A whole winter spent in a freezer," Sam said. "Can you imagine?"

"I know, but it's not like they knew they were in a freezer. At least he killed them before putting them in."

"Doesn't it bother you that we knew him?"

"But we didn't—not really. I talked to him once, I think." I took a swig of my coffee and it made me shudder.

"But we went to the same parties. We've been in a room with him. How many people watching the news right now can say that?"

I wasn't thinking about the trial on the day Camilla went missing. I was thinking about my conversation with Sam *about* the trial, which wasn't quite the same thing. I was certain—the trial wasn't distracting me. I was cold. I couldn't light my cigarette because the wind was blowing too hard. Sam didn't know that I smoked in front of Camilla; I always made sure that her jacket smelled sweet like her and not like me before I brought her back home. We agreed that it would be our secret. To be clear, it didn't feel like I was asking Camilla to keep secrets for me. She didn't mind. Andy MacArthur's secrets were another story altogether. It was all relative. Camilla sat on the swing set, somehow impervious to the cold that must have been creeping through the seams of her snow pants. I felt snot freezing around the edges of my nostrils.

I really had only spoken to Andy once. I thought back and tried to make the conversation remarkable; I replayed it, hoped to colour it so that I had a hunch about him, about what he was, but I couldn't and I didn't.

Before Andy was arrested, Camilla and I were waiting for a bus to take us to the mall. I had her tucked against my side, more for my warmth than for hers. In hindsight, I should have felt relief that nothing had happened to Camilla, but he would never have hurt her—all of his victims were over the age of twenty-five.

We were shielded from the wind in the bus shelter, but the cold had a way of working into my bones no matter how much money I spent on long underwear or flannel lined jeans.

I watched as Andy came into the shelter with us and stood at the furthest edge. I tried to remember who spoke first. I think he must have begun the conversation when he recognized me beneath my parka and scarf.

"Cold, huh?" he'd said.

"Tell me about it."

A pause.

"I like the snow," Camilla chimed in with the childish assumption that Andy was a friendly man. On the outside, I suppose he seemed to be. Children and dogs are supposedly good judges of character, but I guess we can all be fooled.

Neither of us said anything for a moment until he spoke again.

"I'm sorry to hear about you and Tom. You seemed happy at Alex's party a few months ago."

I remember being caught off guard, but only slightly. I didn't remember seeing him at Alex's party. Still, nothing about our conversation felt remotely personal. Maybe it was his delivery. The words came out like a script or a speech-to-text app that was trying its best to be authentically human.

"It was for the best," I said.

The number 9 bus rounded the corner and he hiked the strap of his messenger bag higher onto his shoulder.

"This is me," he said. Before he turned to go, he added, "let me know if you want to get coffee sometime."

I think I nodded at him, but I was distracted by the cold and I couldn't feel my toes and I was fishing in my purse for a moderately used Kleenex to give Camilla. Her nose was dripping and if I didn't give her something to wipe with, she would spread it on her scarf.

"I'll see you around," he said before getting on the bus without looking back.

A week later, I received a message from Andy restating his invitation to coffee. Before I knew why, I'd messaged him back and agreed to meet him the next week at the Lazy Loaf. Even now, I'm not sure why I agreed. I wasn't lonely—I was just sick of winter.

We were going to meet at the café since neither of us had a car. I waited at the bus stop for twenty-five minutes before the bus arrived, but within moments, we were marooned on a median in the road that had been hidden beneath fresh snow. The driver. told us all to stay on the bus while he called for another driver to pick us up. I used the last of my data to message Andy and let him know I'd be late, but by the time a second bus arrived to help us, he messaged me and said he had to get going, he had other business to attend to. He said we would reschedule.

I can't help but wonder what would have happened if I'd actually made it. Would I have ended up in his freezer waiting for the ground to thaw? I stopped myself before I could picture what sex might have been like with Andy.

The cold was making my memories more vivid and I realized my eyes were shut. I don't know how long they were closed, but my eyelashes crunched slightly when I blinked. I turned back to the swing set where Camilla had been twisting the chains to spin in circles, but she was gone. I searched the playground for her yellow jacket, which should have stood out against the snow. If she'd left any footprints, the wind had blown snow over them and there was no way to tell if there was one set or two. I wanted to run and get help, but I needed to stay in case she came back. I knew she would jump out any second, yell *Boo* and I would take her home and we could warm up before Sam came back. Her momentary disappearance would be our secret. Ten minutes passed. Then twenty-five. Then an hour. Then two. The chains on the swing set swayed in the wind. For a moment, I thought, *He took her. He really did it.* I knew he was in custody but I thought back to that day in the bus shelter. Had I shielded her enough? Had I handed Camilla over to him?

After Camilla was found, shivering but alive, the police took us to the station and fed her a ham sandwich and a cup of hot chocolate. They gave me black coffee in a paper cup that seemed about to split at the seams. The bandage on Camilla's head was the size of a coffee coaster—one of her braids had gotten entangled in a branch as she'd trekked through the trees near the playground. It ripped from her scalp as she pulled away. She said she was following a fox to its den in the hopes she might find cubs. Everything was so white. She got lost. When Sam arrived, she didn't look at me—she hugged her daughter carefully so she wouldn't tug on her delicate and damaged scalp.

I called Sam's name, but she didn't look up. Instead, Camilla turned and tried to come back to me, but her mother's grip on the yellow jacket tightened. I watched Sam walk out the door without looking back.

I didn't get to leave for another hour. When the police asked me question after question, I told them what I had told Sam on the phone: Camilla was sitting on the swing set and then she simply wasn't.

Nectar and Nickel

Let me tell you a story: my mother will say she's a liar *and my father will say* she remembers things that never happened, *but you and I know that isn't true. Before I tell you, pick up a pair of scissors, or a pen, or a branch, or a flower stem—something to play with when you don't want to meet my eyes. Unhinge the wasps from your insides before their black venom seeps through.*

◂◂◂◂◂◂

We moved away from my home when I was nine years old (I still maintain that it's my home even though I've lived in many places since). Our house was sturdy and covered in a perpetual layer of dust from the dirt path that wound down the road in coils until it reached our front door. The dust snuck through the cracks in the walls and windows when the wind blew. Until that year, nine had been my favourite age to live.

When I wrote the number 9, the circle closed around me in an embrace and the line held strong like a stem, thorny and rooted in my mother's garden. I pictured the number hanging from the ceiling, suspended by its own circle. When I held up my fingers to show my age, one hand was fully occupied with five fingers, while the other held one finger behind. If I wanted to, I could unfurl that thumb from where it rested on my palm and convince the world that I was ten years old.

It all changed when we moved and number nine became an abscess. The suspended circle wound itself into a noose encircling my stomach and neck and the stick stood like a crooked tombstone. When I used my fingers, my thumb was immobilized, as if locked in tar against my sweating palm. I could fool no one and the world knew it.

The man to your left is my father. He pours himself a glass of sherry each night and before he takes a sip, he slides one finger into the glass and dabs his fingertip across his lower lip. He doesn't know that I watch him (he is watching me now). He worries, but not for my sake. He sees me writing and he knows what stories I could tell and he worries that someday, I might.

The day we left home, I dug up the wooden box my father buried in the garden plot beside the back door. I had no garden tools, because my mother had already packed them away, and the dirt stuck to the pink flesh below my fingernails. When I found the box, I rapped my knuckles on the top as if I were knocking on a door, but no one answered. I pulled it from the earth; the newly discovered space exposed an array of worms and insects below. I left the insects alone and watched them bury deeper into the earth, then replaced the dirt over this space so that they would not dry out and die. I held the box on my lap as its moistness seeped from the wooden bottom, soaking through the front of my dress.

My father had nailed the box shut with industrial force. The top finally loosened and I could pull the length of the nails from the damp wood, curling my fingers around rusted metal. When I lifted the lid, I found him poised exactly as I'd remembered. His eyes and parts of his cheeks had sunken, his whiskers were gone, but his paws were curled below his chin, bone showing through the patches of fur that still remained. I ran a hand down the side of his body and felt my hand covered in a slick coating that glistened in the sun. He had been below the earth for two winters and one spring, and it had taken a toll on his small body. I'd asked father to carry him out of the house feet first. I stopped our kitchen clock when he died (mother started it again within moments). Putting the lid back on the box, I decided to keep him on the carpeted floor of our car for the duration of the drive.

The woman sitting to your right is my mother. This morning she pricked me with a sewing needle while trying to take in the waist of my dress. She already knows that I'll be writing this down; she tells me not to get too fanciful, she warns you that I tell lies. My pen leaks and that is why this page bloats with watered marks. I do not cry. I am not a child.

My parents loaded the truck with the skeletons of our dressers and bookshelves. I walked through our empty home and saw spiders scuttle across the floorboards, leaving their webs empty except for the flies they'd bound with string. *The flies were naughty; their whey was cold. The girls were grotty, filling bowls with mold.* I have to assume the spiders had lived with us always, but they had nowhere to hide once my parents started packing. The house smelled of damp and I tried to keep that smell in the front of my head. I could hear my parents calling my name from outside, but I blocked out the chattering voices to focus on sensations, immediate ones that I could easily forget if I wasn't careful. I rubbed my hands together, grinding dirt into my palms the way my mother rubbed creams into her skin. She worried about drying out and did this four or five times a day. Mother was even more worried than usual—after the bodies were found in the earth next door, she insisted we had to move. I didn't see why we had to leave. That happened in the other house—not in mine.

I saw the bugs gliding from one corner of the room to the other. I noted the small, circular burn mark on the hardwood floor where I'd left a candle burning. I focused on the doorway, the overhang of which had always been slightly crooked. I cupped my hands, put them against the wall and breathed in to capture the scent of this home. My parents stood in the doorway and watched, my father with one hand tightly gripped on my mother's powder dry elbow. My mother put her hand on her forehead to radiate heat into herself. My father tried to smile without turning up the corners of his lips. When they recall that day, they say I was sniffing old paint fumes before we got in the car and drove to a better house. When I recall that day, I remember breathing in my last clean breath of air.

Let me tell you a story: a fox saunters through your front door with a sewing box full of ribbon and scissors. He tells you to pick the longest piece, but you cannot measure them and you cannot touch them. If you reach out a hand, he will leave and he will not come back. You choose a strand of yellow ribbon, because the yellow is the same yellow of the peeling wallpaper at your home. He leaves and takes his box of ribbon with him, closing the door with the back of his haunch, the scissors rattling in their compartments. You were wrong.

We arrived at our new house four hours after leaving home. I kept one foot on top of the box while we drove, in case the cat got any ideas about leaving, and mother and father never knew he was there. When we arrived, my father put his key in the lock, but it didn't open. He jiggled the key around, muttering *damn* under his breath, and blaming the dampness for the shifting wooden frame. Red creases and streaks crossed his palm from where he'd tried to force the key to turn. When the door finally unlocked, it swung inward and opened to an unlit entryway. "Welcome Home," my parents said. As my father searched for a light switch, I turned toward the drive and wandered with the wooden box under my arm. To the left of our house stood a crooked tree with a hollow hole in its centre. Dried leaves gathered at the base of the tree, dead and crumbling. I moved my hands to my neck, shifting my hair out of the way to unhinge the clasp of my necklace. The chain slid through my fingers the way butter might, weighted by the locket at the end. I placed it in the hollow of the tree to claim it as my own then walked through the open door of the new house.

We'd only been in the house half an hour when a boy with dirt on his cheeks came to see us. I watched him from the front room window before he knocked on the door. He'd peeked into the hollow of the tree and had taken my locket from inside, wrapping it around his fingers before slipping it into his pants pocket. The movers and my parents were still shuffling around me with straps, pieces of furniture and boxes.

Mother came to the door when he knocked and gauged us to be around the same age. She called me to say hello to our new neighbour. She was wrong. I was nine and he was eleven. When I told them both that I didn't want to go outside, he didn't flinch, but mother pinched my back in a way that the boy couldn't see. I turned around to go up the new stairs, but he called my name and told me that he lived five minutes down the road in the house with a blue door and a white awning. If I walked toward the oak tree at the end of the lane, I would be going towards him. He didn't tell me his name as he turned on his heel and left. I wondered, in the cyclical nature of things, if there would be bodies in his backyard someday. It would be fitting if we ran from one house with bodies next door to another. I watched him walk to the end of our new driveway. He kicked up dust as he went; he didn't pick up his feet when he walked. I waited a few moments, my hands gripping the doorframe on either side, and then my mother pinched me until I walked out the door with the wooden box under my arm.

This boy in front of you has dirt on his face. He lifted the lid from the box and stroked the body with clean fingers. He brushed one of the rib bones and I pictured him brushing mine. Before he knew it, the cat jumped out, scratched his dirty face, and chased him home. Wasps were spinning and spiraling in a line. We never saw the boy again. When the cat returned, he wore my locket around his neck. We sat on a stump and we ate whey and we were alone.

Garden Bed

WINIFRED

sections her garden into quarters: perennials, biennials, annuals, and herbs. Her dress pools around her ankles as the grass digs into her bare knees; sharp blades cut her skin. She leans back on her heels with a trowel in one hand and a pile of dirt in the other, feeling her palms tickle with the legs of invisible insects. She plans to plant daisies, Sweet Williams, hydrangeas, and peonies, knowing that they return year after year regardless of hostile conditions. A box no larger than her fist sits beside her with a stinging nettle settled against the lid.

THE FOX

watches the woman with the trowel dig in the dirt. He has smelled her many times. Her face is wet but she smells like calmness. She doesn't know that he has marked this spot. He will dig up her flowers and carry them away with him.

HARRY

sits at the kitchen table remembering their conversation: *these things happen,* he'd said, *there isn't much left to do.* He refrained from saying *no use crying over spilt milk,* recognizing the callousness she'd rightly accuse him of. But he also heard his mother's voice creeping into the phrase the way weeds circle around roots in the garden and take hold. From his seat at the table, he watches her in the garden with her back to him. Her hair blows out in wisps like dandelion seeds when the breeze pushes her. It's too quiet in the kitchen and he can't get the sound of his mother's voice to leave his ears. He turns on the radio. From the speakers, a woman's voice sings: *a fox is a wolf who sends flowers.* He turns the radio off.

WINIFRED

deadheads the remnants of last year's growth and pulls decaying flowers out at the roots. As they release and give way, she places them in a pile on the grass next to her. She tugs the dandelions and weeds that grow in seemingly spontaneous patterns. She tried to plant flowers and bulbs in pots for inside the house, but the leaves dried even though she watered and pruned. She lifts the earth with the trowel as pressure builds on a blister growing on her right thumb. No one told her how much it would hurt.

HARRY

remembers the way her fingers ran around the rim of the wine glass at the restaurant. She had dipped her finger in the water and traced the lip with her wet fingertip. The glass vibrated until it sang. He'd finished his glass of brandy and swirled the remnants of ice cubes around the bottom. He'd finished his drink but he kept bringing the glass to his lips, forgetting that it was empty. The couples around them turned when Winifred's glass sang and she stopped, feeling their eyes digging into her skin. *It's just the way it goes sometimes,* he'd said, trying to fill the space that remained in the absence of sound. He sat with his middle and pointer finger against his mouth, as if he were holding an invisible cigar.

THE FOX

moves a few feet closer; the woman has not seen him yet. He
is wary of dried leaves crunching under his paws. He lost the
tip of his tail in the cold and he cannot find it. Slowly, he lies
down on his belly to feel the sun warming his back. He yawns
and decides to sleep. She will still be there when he wakes up.

WINIFRED

has already packed. The box with the stinging nettle is her
last step. She has not prayed since her years in Catholic
school and she does not pray now. She says only to
herself, *I gave all to you,* and blows the nettle from the
lid. She empties the contents of the box into the space
she's opened in the earth; she lifts her trowel and shovels
in wet dirt. With mud caked beneath her fingers, she
packs down the earth and wipes her hands on her dress.

THE FOX

waits until she stands up and goes inside. She comes back out
and gets in the car. When he is sure she's gone, he digs in the
earth until his paws are blackened like her hands. He thinks
that maybe the tip of his tail is underneath. He marks all four
corners of the garden to make it his own and strides away
with plants and seeds between his teeth. His tail is not here.

Bruised Plums

She keeps having dreams about her grandmother—that she arrives uninvited to a dinner party—that she finds her, rifling through the apple bins in the produce aisle—that her grandmother turns up at her own funeral with a bouquet of white lilies and potato salad in a store-bought container. She understands that none of these can happen because her grandmother's funeral took place two weeks ago, and the lilies have already been laid in front of the head stone. Besides, Plum knows her grandmother would never bring anything to a funeral that was store bought.

As she reaches into her purse for her keys, she feels her phone vibrate in the back pocket of her jeans. Her screen shows an unknown number and location. Before her grandmother died, she would have ignored a call like this, but she worries about missing calls from relatives whose numbers she doesn't recognize or whose names she doesn't know. She's already had strangers arriving on her doorstep expecting shelter and comfort after the loss of her grandmother and guardian. Plum presses *Accept Call* and lifts the phone to her ear.

Hello?

At first, there's only silence, then Plum hears a growing, crackling static. She waits a few more moments, rummaging through her purse with her free hand, and then tries again with more emphasis on the second syllable, as though this makes her sound more in control.

Hello?

The static drifts in and out of Plum's hearing until she finally presses *End Call*. She knows she needs a new phone; the device is ancient and overheats when she keeps it in her pocket for too long. She holds the phone in one hand, pushes her house key into the lock with the other, then moves through the doorway. Her landline begins to ring as she closes the door behind her.

The townhouse has been in the family for eighty-seven years with the occasional non-family member occupant in the forties. Plum's grandmother, Delilah, lived there for sixty-seven years. Plum has lived there with her for the past twenty of those. Her grandmother kept the house in "guest ready" condition, cleaning once a week, having the furnace checked once a year, and never letting water sit around the taps. A few years back, Plum's grandmother noticed a thumping sound when she turned off the taps in the kitchen and bathrooms. The house had always made noise, creaking and the like, but this was different. If Plum stood in the basement when her grandmother shut off a tap on the third floor, she felt the walls rattle and heard the sounds of pipes shifting on every level until the sound reached her. When she was younger, Plum ran down the stairs to the basement to do whatever needed to be done as quickly as possible. She twitched every time she felt something brush against her arm, as if stringy fingers were reaching out to grab at her. It was usually insulation that had loosened from the wall, but Plum ran regardless.

Her grandmother tried turning all of the taps on at once to let air out of the pipes, but the rattling and thumping continued. The sound didn't bother Plum much, but Delilah called a plumber from the yellow pages. He arrived with a stethoscope in his bag and he instructed Plum to turn each tap in the house off and on. He pressed the stethoscope against the walls, listening for possible leaks or damage. This lasted for hours while her grandmother observed from the living room. Finally, when he'd pressed his stethoscope against each section of wall, he sat down in the living room, looking a little too large for Delilah's armchair. Plum and her grandmother sat on the couch. He took a deep breath before he began.

I'm afraid I've got some bad news. The house is inoperable—you have water hammer.

Both Plum and her grandmother wanted to laugh at the gravity of the plumber's prognosis, but they had to feign genuineness to avoid offending him.

Are you sure?

They already knew they'd be seeking a second opinion.

I'm afraid so, ma'am.

With that, the house groaned, as it occasionally did, and the plumber packed up his tools. He shook their hands and apologized, again, as he walked out the door.

Plum returns home with her arms full of grocery bags. The plastic handles dig into her wrists, leaving pink grooves against her skin. She wrestles with the grocery bags and her purse to get to her keys when she hears the sound of creaking wheels behind her.

Are you new here?

Plum turns around, bags in hand, to see her neighbour from the townhouse opposite and one over from hers. He rides out to meet her on an electric scooter, the same brand and model her grandmother had owned. Plum knows by now that the man never wears shirts, and she is already too well acquainted with the curves and crevasses of his midsection.

No, I've lived here for twenty years. You'd probably remember my grandmother, Delilah. She lived here for longer than I have.

Plum's grocery bags are cutting into her wrists, chafing off layers of skin as she sweats in the summer heat.

Are you sure? he asked. *I could have sworn this unit had been empty for years.*

Plum's phone begins to vibrate in her back pocket.

I guess I don't go out very much.

Plum chuckles, proving to herself as much as him that she's only joking. He wears a "Hello My Name Is" nametag on his bare chest, with an empty space where his name should be.

Regardless, she knows his name is Alfred.

Well, welcome to the neighbourhood anyway.

Alfred puts his chair in reverse and backs into the darkness of his garage. Plum knows they will have the same exchange next week. She doesn't tell him that there is, as he remembered, a unit that's been empty for years, but it's beside his and not across. He housed his aging mother there before she passed away. The unit has remained furnished, but uninhabited for eighteen years. With the right lighting, Plum can usually see portions of the kitchen from her dining room and bedroom windows.

Plum's phone has stopped vibrating; she missed the call. She hoists her grocery bags up higher and glides her key into the lock. Pressing the door with the bottom of her shoe, she enters her empty home.

In the winter that Plum was ten years old, she was woken one night by a long, screaming string of words uttered outside her bedroom window. She sat up in bed, blood rushing to her ears, and tried to piece the words into a coherent sentence. She was fairly certain she'd heard them spoken out loud, but as her eyes adjusted to the dark and her ears to the silence, she wondered if she'd dreamt them.

Don't let him get away. Please. Don't let him take her away.

Plum was suddenly cold, realizing that she'd forgotten to close her window before falling asleep. She reached her hand to the curtains and saw small patches of ice against the wooden sill in crystalline clusters. She scraped them with her nails, carving patterns and spirals into the thin layer of ice. The sheer portion of her blind had blown out from behind her bedframe and was strewn across the room, as if the force of the woman's voice had driven it from the wall. She pushed a button on her watch, which told her it was 2:37 a.m. Plum reached under her bed for her journal and her pen. Illuminated by the light of her watch, she wrote the time and copied down the words she'd heard outside.

It only occurred to her while she wrote that she should tell her grandmother. As she got to her feet, a light snapped on in the hallway. Plum could see the shadows of her grandmother's slippers in the crack below her door and she could hear her grandmother's voice relaying over the telephone the words Plum had heard outside.

She couldn't hear a responding voice on the other end of the line like she normally could. Plum lifted her blind and looked out at the drive below. The scream must have come from a long way away. She didn't see anyone moving in the light from the streetlamps. As she shifted her gaze upward, she saw the briefest flash of light in the empty townhouse across from hers, as quick as an extinguishing bulb. The flash was too brief to be able to see who was in the apartment, but Plum could distinguish the outline of a figure standing at the kitchen window.

The telephone call was short and there were no more screams outside the window that night. In the morning, her grandmother made hot cocoa with breakfast and asked her how she'd slept. She said *just fine* as she looked out the kitchen window to the townhouse across. The blinds were as they'd always been, hanging slightly crooked on the left side, streaming light against the kitchen table where no one sat for eighteen years. Plum inspected the front of the house again when she left for school but could find no trace of a figure in the window.

Plum removes last week's apples from her fruit bowl, taking the brown, bruised ones to throw away and leaving only those that are spotless. She'd gone to the grocery store since her fruit had begun to rot overnight. Plum assumes some sort of fruit fly or pesticide must have turned them brown quicker than usual. Untying the plastic bags, she washes each apple by hand and lays them out in her fruit bowl to dry. At the very bottom of the bowl, she finds a sweet potato she'd forgotten to use, propped beneath her new batch of bananas and her oranges. Lifting it to inspect the damage, she sees the potato has grown, sprouting stems through the skin that look like tentacles to Plum. She uses the bag from the apples to wrap up the potato and throws it into the bin before its disturbance can turn the air in the kitchen rancid.

Once the groceries are put away, Plum sets about cleaning. She tries to tidy without disturbing the books, photo frames, and papers strewn throughout the townhouse. Her grandmother's obituary still sits, cut from the newspaper, on the table between cups of cold coffee and books with dog-eared corners. Her grandmother's copy of *As I lay Dying* is still on the table, with a bookmark at page 169. Plum would like to read the book but cannot fathom moving the bookmark or disturbing the pages her grandmother's fingers last touched. Plum feels drained as she lowers herself into her grandmother's armchair and closes her eyes. She has not slept soundly since the funeral and most mornings, the phone rings around five even though it's been disconnected from the wall.

A crackling static fills Plum's ears, pushing into the sides of her head in waves of vibrations. She wakes disoriented to find herself in the armchair and not in her bed. Stretching and trying to work the static from her brain, she stands and opens the window, but the blood rushes to her head and blocks her vision for a few moments.

She's not sure how long she's been asleep, but the sun has gone down and all seems to be quiet outside. Rubbing the heel of her palm into her forehead, Plum closes her eyes. The static in her ears feels like helium, pushing out and lifting her in all directions. Her phone vibrates again in her back pocket, but she makes no motion to pick it up. This vibration feels the same as the others coursing through her body. She hears thuds in the walls and the sound of trickling water from the upper floors. She must have left the tap running upstairs, but she doesn't remember turning it on.

The LED light on the landline blinks to tell Plum that there's a voicemail, but she doesn't want to listen to it. She needs fresh air and to get away from the house.

The static suddenly clears and a blanket of silence surrounds her, with only the crackling sound of a fireplace she didn't light. She sees a flicker of brightness in her peripheral vision. As she turns, she realizes that the brightness emanates from the upper floor of the townhouse across the street. She watches as it lights and dims three more times. On the fourth, it flickers and stays lit to illuminate a kitchen table from above. This time, Plum does not see a figure at the window, but instead, three figures sitting at the kitchen table eating dinner. She doesn't recognize two of them, but she recognizes the third, carving a leg of lamb, as her grandmother. Plum takes her overheating phone and runs to the door as the crackling in the fireplace and the pounding in the walls begin again and static fills her mind. Her heart clatters in her chest as she runs down the stairs. She tries to reconcile the familiar image of her grandmother in the kitchen with what she knows to be true. Her grandmother has been buried. Her grandmother is underground in a casket and she is also across the street carving lamb. As soon as Plum opens the door, her head clears. She closes the door behind her, but when she turns back to the townhouse, the light in the kitchen flickers and dims again. She can no longer discern kitchen fixtures, just the dirty window frames the same as her own. Plum can see nothing in the blackened window. She stands alone in the light of a streetlamp. Alfred's *Hello my name is* nametag drifts across the pavement to land at her feet.

Red Strings

eight: what are you looking forward to?

I stand at the edge of the barn and watch the oak tree go up first. From where I'm standing, it looks like the tree is spitting its leaves, trying to save them from the wreckage. The trunk splits down its center, shuddering more leaves out into the air. Fall is a beautiful time for it all to burn. The fire spreads. The tendrils of smoke drift across the field and latch onto the siding of the farmhouse. Not long now. There are no more footprints lining the way from the oak tree to the farm, but now oak leaves litter the ground and the low riding smoke snakes between the two. I try to clean my hands, but the gasoline spreads across my palms and seeps into the fine lines. It pools under my fingernails and I hear the crackle of our radio from inside. A news report about colour blindness, I think. I think about what Grandma used to say as I watch the tree shudder in the smoke. *We don't know what it's like to be the ocean.*

one: what do you think brings you here?

Grandpa says the people in this town honk their horns to talk to each other; one short honk to say hello, three times to warn that police are down the road with breathalyzers, and one long for when the hockey team wins. Grandpa says we should honk our horn when we turn the blind corner just before the farm; that way whatever's on the other side knows we're there. Grandpa says you don't want to miss something just because you didn't listen. Grandpa says if you see a kid on a bike honking their plastic, clown horn, you better smile at them, too. Grandpa says they might squint at you from under the visors of their helmets, and you'll remember when your muscles were loose and lanky like theirs. Grandpa says never forget that. Grandpa holds the horn down the whole time he rounds the corner. Grandpa doesn't slow down, because he has flowers in the trunk and wants to get home to us as fast as he can.

two: what is the problem from your viewpoint?

Grandpa sweeps his hands across the maple tabletop and sends the funeral home forms floating down onto the linoleum. I think he wanted them to fall faster, like pots and pans might have. He wanted them to crash and dent the floor, but they just float down until they coat the floorboards like petals. I think he wanted Grandma to be cremated here at the farm, but the funeral home won't let him. I don't want him to know that I saw him throw the paperwork; I keep my eyes just above my Maya Angelou book. I used to close my right eye and walk around the house to see what Grandpa saw when he walked. He told me what he has is called Glaucoma and there was nothing we can do about it. I found the word in my science books and saw we could fix it if we went to the doctor fast enough. It wouldn't go away, but we could make it better for him.

When I told Grandpa, he said *like hell I'm going to the doctor. know what they'll do to me? they'll take it out. i'd rather have a bad eye in my head than a bad eye floating in a jar.* All I could picture after that was an eyeball floating in the center of a jar and Grandpa walking around with a hole in his head like an open mouth that never spoke. He rakes the forms up off the floor and walks out the door. I run to the window to watch him leave. The cat follows him out the door, and they leave two pairs of footprints in the snow. Grandpa's footprints are straight and evenly spaced but the cat's footprints snake around his like smoke tendrils.

three: what makes the problem better?

We had to burn the cat. Grandpa was turning the blind corner and didn't see her in time to stop. He honked as he turned, but the cat didn't move. The screen door creaked, and he came in with a brown lump in his arms. He carried her the same way he carried firewood; her straight body leaned against his arm and shoulder. Grandpa settled her down, packed her in hay, poured the gasoline and lit the match. My eyes watered with familiar heat and it all sounded like crackling leaves. We had just lost the chickens and their ashes were still dissipating. The smell coated my nose and wouldn't leave, no matter how many times I blew into Grandma's handkerchief trimmed with violets. I kept expecting to see it coated in black when I pulled it from my face.

four: and how does that make you feel?

I reach my hand into my pocket to feel for the metal angel that Grandma gave me. I feel its weight in my palm and trace the pressed angel's shape with my fingertip. She kept it in her change purse and almost mistook it for a quarter a few times when she went to the store. I had to tug on the hem of her skirt to get her to notice her mistake. Tugging on her skirt released a puff of old cigarette smoke smell from the fabric. I liked to think that I could associate a time and place with each iteration of smoke. It could have been from her cigarette, sitting at the back of my school gymnasium for the spelling bee. Or it could have been the smoke bouncing off the closed car windows when Grandpa was driving us home.

It could have been the smoke dispersed when she took her scarf off at the front door. It could have been smoke from a forest fire where foxes scampered and birds beat their wings to get away from the flames. Grandma used to say that she hated the smell of old cigarette smoke. I never understood why. Instead, Grandma loved the smell of gasoline. She kept her handkerchief tucked into her sleeve and sometimes loose tissues, too. I used to follow behind her, picking up the ones that dropped to the ground. I followed her trail of tissues and smoke.

five: how are you sleeping?

Grandpa asked me to crack eggs for dinner. We'd been buying eggs from the store since the chickens died. He handed me six eggs from the carton that creaked when he pushed the tabs back into place. Grandpa's hands were big enough that he could hold four eggs in each hand. I took one egg and cracked it against the side of the chipped glass bowl. I half-cracked the egg, creating little rifts in the white shell and then had to peel bits of the membrane back to fully open it. The yolk hung in the center of the bowl, swimming in the rest of the egg white. I reached for the next egg when I noticed a spot in the bowl. A red smear like string clung to the yolk's center. My stomach turned and I cupped my mouth with one hand and pushed the bowl across the table with the other. Grandpa noticed. *it's just a little blood. come on, you won't even taste it once it's cooked.*

Grandpa took the bowl to his side of the table and mixed the egg with a whisk. The red stretched into a thin strand pulled taut, then finally yielded, breaking apart and dissipating into the rest of the egg. I closed my eyes and waited for my stomach to turn itself right side up.

six: when did you start feeling unwell?

I keep the cat's ashes in a box under the kitchen sink. I haven't decided where to scatter them yet. She liked to watch birds under the oak tree; maybe I'll scatter them there. I used to go down to the oak tree with Grandma. Grandpa had gone into the city and we were going to have a picnic. She held a basket of apples in one of her hands and my hand in her other. Halfway down the hill she took her hand from mine to cough into her handkerchief. She tried to tuck it back into her sleeve before I could see, but it was covered in red strings, each one wrapping around the violets, crystalline, like a mosaic.

seven: do you ever feel ashamed?

There was a girl named Jubilee who lived down the road from us. I told her that Grandpa died too, and she told me that everything happens for a reason. She said that her dad died in a motorcycle crash and that it was her fault. She said it happened because she'd lied to her mom about the cigarettes she'd stolen from her purse. She said my cat and my grandparents died because my mom and dad weren't married when they had me. Her voice was gentle and lilting, which made me think that she really believed this. I took one of Grandma's cigarettes out of my pocket, put it between my lips and left Jubilee making crop circles in the red gravel with the tips of her shoes.

I walked back to the farm, and laid Grandma's violet-trimmed handkerchief on Grandpa's chest. I'm starting to understand why Grandma loved the smell of gasoline.

Home Burial

Open me carefully. The envelope arrived in Emilie's mailbox at three in the afternoon, two hours after her discharge from the hospital and one hour before the letter burned in her fireplace between two sprigs of rosemary. She knew the exact time of the letter's arrival because her mother had built a sturdy, wooden mailbox with a lid made of oak to nail to the front door. Her mother had also made a broom of birch and twine for sweeping the front porch. Her aunt had sent her home with tomatoes and sprigs of rosemary. Her mother had sent her home with a warning and a prayer that she would not bleed. The sound of the mailbox had roused her from sleep and she woke with the chalk taste of antacids on her lips.

Emilie had barely slept in the hospital. The tubes, checkups, and yelling made it impossible. Still, the worst was the constant buzz of the muted TV with blue crackles down the centre of the screen. She watched news programs, the mouths of the anchors moving too fast for her to read, and listened to the beeps and drips around the room. In her armchair, she ran a finger along the incision mark on her stomach and fingered the stitches. A piece of her had vanished, but she couldn't remember what it felt like to be full. The piece had already become something else, somewhere else.

She wouldn't describe it like a phantom appendage—just a phantom.

When the mailbox shut, she'd been dreaming about spiders closing in around the periphery of her vision. As a child, when she saw the spiders, she knew something was coming. The family cat would die, the boy down the road would descend into a fit of seizures, someone would be arrested, and her neighbour would be in a car accident. There was always something coming. The spiders usually came to steal the letters from her books.

Occasionally, they'd leave the title on her page, but more often than not, they took every consonant and vowel. Her mother gave Emilie herbs to settle her nerves and taught her to put her hands over her eyes when she saw the spiders coming. When she reached sixteen, the spiders came in such large swarms that she couldn't do anything about them. She lay down on the floor with an empty, open book beside her and stared at the stucco ceiling as it slowly closed over with black spots. Her mother stood over her, moving her lips but Emilie could not hear her words. She did not see the spiders again for many years. This calmed her at first, but she missed them in the end.

ᴧᐸᐸᐸᐸᐸᐤ

Before she opened the letter, she placed it on the wooden table in front of her, feeling the folds and creases. She ran a finger along the edge, not hard enough to cut herself, but with a light pressure. When she touched the printed letters, the ink smudged across the pad of her finger and bled out into the white of the envelope. She picked at the remnants of blue polish on her nails. She managed to scrape a nail from the bottom to the tip in one piece. It sat beside the letter, transected from her hands. The trace of colour that remained made her fingernails look like something drowned and dead. She didn't mind this. *Open me carefully.*

The letters are printed in black marker with the curving slant of familiar handwriting; printed with the kind of ink that bleeds out the sides of individual letters, absorbed into pores of the paper. She wondered if these words would transfer to the pages inside, weeping through the white sheets and onto the table. Her palms smeared with streaks of black. She left the letter in the envelope and sipped from the mug of rainwater her mother collected.

The Fever Dream (in the House)

Something Blue

You sit across from me at the kitchen table, a cup of cold coffee in your hands, a furrow between your brows, sweat stains beneath the armpits of your tee-shirt (I've told you before that grey shows sweat like nothing else, but you don't seem to care). I am picking my cuticles, scraping my nails against the slight scab that forms around my injection site and I resist the temptation to tug at my eyelashes. My abdomen cramps and I try not to show it.

Since you weren't there, let me tell you what happened this morning: when I arrived at the clinic, I pulled my sleeve over my hand to open the door. You never know what might be hiding on high contact surfaces. Actually, *you* might not know, but I do. Researchers in Worcester found one thousand three hundred and twenty-three different bacterial colonies across twenty-seven doorhandles. Generally, people think that bathrooms are the most germ-infested place in the house, but most bacterial studies find yeast and mold on the remote control, phone handset, and computer keyboard. We clean our bathrooms with some regularity, but we never clean the remote control. You don't remember? I've told you about this over and over—when you reach your hand into the bowl of popcorn, touch the remote to change the channel, and then put your hand back in the bowl.

You never listen to me.

I was about to open the door to the clinic when something on the grass caught my eye. A grey spot that stood out in all that green. A robin—belly up, legs bent, slightly deflated. I pushed disgust down my throat and tried not to think of this as an omen.

But how could it not be?

Up the elevator, past the dental lab that smells like paint thinner, through another door, and into a lobby where every piece of furniture is a different shade of brown. I walk through the lobby, past the nurses' break room, and into the treatment room where chairs are set up in a wide U-shape. You've never made time to come with me for an infusion, so I'll describe the room to you as though I'm still there. Sometimes I feel like I never really leave. The chairs are full on either side, so I am obligated to take the chair in the middle, which is the worst, because it's directly in front of the TV. Usually, it's *The Young and the Restless* or a similar soap opera, but today, it is a news report of a double homicide in Red Deer. The screen freezes for a moment on a shot of a Toyota Corolla, blood splattered across the hood, a crack bursting like a spider web on the windshield. A nurse grabs the remote to change the channel and I wonder if it has ever been disinfected.

In this seat, I feel like I'm being watched on all sides, but I know that no one else even sees me. They come in, get hooked up to their IVs, pull out their books, or their crosswords, or their phones, and tune out the rest of the world.

Drip.

Do you remember our conversation this morning before I went in? I woke up to hair plastered across the back of my neck with sweat. When I opened my eyes, you were already sitting up in bed, which was a surprise, since you'd spent the night on the couch. You scrolled through your phone. I tried to stretch my legs, casually, as if I barely noticed you'd come back to bed, but a cramp burst across my right calf and I winced. I remembered that I'd been forgetting to take my supplements.

"Everything okay?" you asked.

"What time is it?" A question with a question.

"A little bit after eight."

"Eight? I don't normally sleep past six."

"Well, today you did."

Even as I was waking up, I remember thinking: are you going to say anything? Do you regret what you said to me last night? When you said, you could never forgive me, do you picture that as a final decision? Or one in evolution?

I pulled the covers over my head and thought about the dream I'd had. If you and I were speaking normally, I would have told you about it. But as it was, I kept it to myself. I was part of a long line of people marching towards something, but I wasn't sure what. No one spoke, it was just one foot in front of the other. I remember a pain in my right foot, and when I stepped out of the line to look down, I discovered that I had stepped on a nettle and my foot was bleeding. The blood was running down the arch of my foot in a slow trickle and I'd lost my place in line. When I looked up, a skeletal face was looking back, beckoning me onward. I came back in line and felt a hand on my shoulder. When I turned to see whose it was, I screamed because there was no skin covering the hand. It was only bones, joints, and bits of gristly tissue holding it all together. And then I woke up. I wonder if I actually screamed out loud; maybe that's why you came back to bed. Or maybe it's because you've forgiven me.

I don't know if I've forgiven you.

I pulled the covers off and found the sheets stained with blood. I checked my foot first in case I'd actually cut myself in the night, but the blood spread out like butterfly wings beneath my hips and I knew exactly what had happened. I knew you'd seen it too. I stood up, patted the duvet down over the blood stain. My appointment was in the next hour. I had to get in the shower, get dressed, eat something. You had turned on the coffee maker, but it must have been hours before because the coffee was strong and cold.

Drip.

"I'll drop you off on my way to work," you said as though you would have come into the clinic if only you didn't have a nine o'clock meeting. I think it scares you—actually, I know it does. You worry that you'll see me in the clinic with an IV in my arm and that you'll never be able to unsee it. The problem, as I see it, is that you don't see *anything* this way. You only see what I did, you only see what's unforgivable, you only see the illusion of health.

"Are you okay getting a cab home?" you asked.

"Yes," I said.

We drove to the infusion centre and you ran a red light. People don't know that the clinic even exists until they need it—most of the patients go for chemo treatments, but some, like me, go to get their immune systems short circuited and rerouted with biologic drugs. I can see that you want to tell me *I know all of this. I know everything about you,* but you don't. I need to tell you this. I receive my medication through an IV in my hand or my arm and I wait while it is pumped into my veins alongside a saline solution.

"I love you," you said, finally. "You'll be fine."

Drip.

"I'll text you when I'm hooked up."

I had a panic attack at my first infusion; I'd thought I was ready but as the nurse inserted the needle into my hand, my vision blacked over, the blood left my face, my heartbeat sounded in my ears, and while another nurse was asking if I was alright, I was underwater. I surfaced long enough to tell the nurse that I felt nauseous and they thrust a kidney pan in my direction into which I promptly vomited. One nurse continued to fiddle with the IV, another brought a bottle of water, and a third pulled the hair from where it was glued to my neck with sweat and put an ice pack at the base of my skull. I tried not to look around but caved and glanced at the other patients. None even looked in my direction. I wondered if any of them had reacted this way at their first infusion or if I alone was an embarrassment to "The Secret Society of the Chronically Ill." They will revoke my membership.

No one else was throwing up or panicking. They were probably going to leave the clinic and drive themselves home after.

Drip.

This morning, I sit down in the chair, remove my shoes, and try to prepare myself, remembering that I practiced my breathing patterns and visualization exercises (I picture a needle as it pierces my skin, a small, straw-like tube as it is inserted into a vein, and blood as it is drained. All routine). As I describe this, I can see you squirming a little even though you try not to show it.

"Willow?" a nurse calls from the doorway and I nod. Today's nurse is one I haven't seen before. Her hair is longer on one side than the other and her scrubs are covered in small kittens playing with balls of yarn. Her nametag says *Cait*.

"And how are we doing today?" Cait asks.

"I'm alright," I tell her. I launch into my preamble. "Since we haven't met before, I just want to let you know that I'm not great with needles. I won't watch what you're doing, and I'd prefer if you didn't describe or walk me through anything. I'll just try to space out and I'll let you do your thing."

"No one likes needles, sweetie."

I feel my eyes narrow when she calls me *sweetie*. Cait leaves the room to mix the medication and when she returns, she holds two bags of fluid, one of which costs a few thousand dollars; the other is a bag of saline solution. She reaches behind me to put the bags on the IV stand, but one drops to the floor (I pray it's the saline solution). Cait drops the bag two more times before I can see which one it is that she's dropping.

"One of those days, you know?" She winks at me, and I try to stop a cringe from showing on my face. When the bags are finally hung properly, she asks me to roll up my sleeves and she checks my forearms and the backs of both hands. In moments like this, I feel like I'm being inspected for butchering and the nurse is deciding on the best cuts. Cait settles on a vein in my left arm near the inner wrist. Before the nurse can insert the needle, she takes vitals: a blood pressure cuff around my arm, a heart rate monitor on my fingertip, and a thermometer in my ear. After disinfecting the skin and laying her tools out on the small plastic table that doubles as an arm for the chair, Cait says, "I'm going to insert the needle now, take a deep breath and count down from three." I feel myself tense as Cait inserts the needle and I hope that the worst is over. I expect to hear the clicks and snaps of the necessary tubes being attached for bloodwork, but Cait only says *hmmm*.

I hear her take a deep breath before she says, "We didn't get a vein there. We'll have to try again." I want to tell her that *you* will have to try again. Cait says *we* as though I am responsible for moving my veins away or being stingy with my blood. I bite my tongue and count to four in time with my inhales and exhales, muttering that I need a minute before another attempt. As Cait sits back, impatient, I have time to notice the tattoos on her wrists, both in cursive script: *It is what it is* on the right wrist and *not my circus not my monkeys* on the left. I take a last sip of water and nod at Cait who sits back a little bit, examining my arm, and says, "Here we go," and I feel the painful prick of skin being punctured and pierced. This one hurts more than the first, as though she has nicked something that shouldn't be touched.

"Nope," Cait says, "that one didn't work either. I think we actually got a valve that time. Do you think you could relax a little? Your nerves are making *me* nervous."

I want to tell her that if nervous patients make her nervous, maybe she should try another profession, like accounting or a topiary business. My phone buzzes against my leg—I hope rather than think it might be a text from you—but it's from my sister, Hollie. *How's the infusion going?* I'll call her and tell her about all of this when I get back home after a bath and a nap. Hollie is probably at work anyway and won't see a message from me for a while. She works at a funeral home and thankfully doesn't tell me what (or who) she's working on.

"Are you ready to try again, my little pincushion?" I bite back the bile I feel rising in my throat, thank myself for having the foresight to only have a light breakfast, and nod. "If this one doesn't work, I'll get someone else to try," Cait says. She asks me to make a fist, which I pump open and closed. Again, my skin is pierced with this piece of metal that is objectively small but feels larger and larger the further in it goes. "Got it!" Cait says and I can't let my guard down just yet, because she still needs to take blood and get the medication hooked up. I don't trust her not to let the needle slide out of my veins like tender meat from a fork. Another minute before I can let myself settle; I can't even think about relaxing until Cait leaves and I'm alone with my IV stand and I can put headphones on and pretend this isn't happening. After Cait has drawn blood, she attaches the IV tube, tapes it against my skin, and tells me she will be back in fifteen minutes to take vitals again. I feel a chill climbing my arms as the medication makes its upward ascent.

I take a picture to show you later, holding up my hand with the IV, the yellow cannula, and the tape over top that reflects the fluorescent lights in the clinic. I send the photo to my sister, *All in. It was a tough one, but I'll tell you about it later.* She sends a heart back and tells me to hang in there. Thankfully, she doesn't send me a photo of her hand because it's probably about to be or just coming out of someone's body cavity. I haven't heard anything from you. An older woman I have seen in the clinic before (her name might be Pippa) settles into the chair next to me and smiles. None of us ask each other what we're here for, but most of the patients have IV bags that say INF. Cait goes up to the woman next to me and asks, "Where do you want to get stabbed today?" Pippa looks over at me with a raised brow and then back to Cait before she points to her left hand. The nurses won't need to speak to me for an hour while the medication drips through my system, so I put on my headphones and press play.

As the nurse sets Pippa up with her IV, I close my eyes. I let the music drip into me in time with my medication. My eyelids flutter and then stay shut.

Drip.

I am walking in a field. Green. Yellow tips on dandelions. Bits of pollen in the air settle across my bare arms. When I look in front of me, I see someone's back. When I look behind, another person, but I can't focus on faces. I'm in some kind of procession—they walk in a straight line. I step to the side to take myself away from the group and something inside me tugs; the sensation is how I imagine an umbilical cord might feel as it's pinched and cut. Not that I would know what that particular sensation feels like. There's only a little bit of pain when I separate, but the group goes on without me and this time, no skeletal hands come to grab me and pull me back in.

I sit cross-legged next to the paved path, while the procession goes on ahead of me. I still can't see their faces because they've turned away and I feel like maybe I've had this dream before. I haven't been here before, I know that much, but something feels uncanny about the procession, the warmth, the tug in my stomach. I lean back a little, resting weight on my palms and tilt my head back as far as it can comfortably go to look up to the sky; I know it's an illusion, but somehow there are two suns, side by side, each warming my face. Perhaps it's my vision tricking me, or maybe there really are two suns. Who am I to say what's real and what isn't?

As I look back down and my vision blots and clears again from staring into the sun, I feel something wet spreading across my left hand. I look down and a gag begins in the back of my throat. My hand has been resting on a dead robin, split open down the middle of its stomach, with three blue eggs, all cracked, peeking from between my fingers. It is wet and the wetness is underneath my fingernails and soaking into my cuticles and running down my arms, gizzards, congealed blood, eggshells, split skin, damp feathers. One of its feet wraps around my ring finger and won't let me go.

I open my eyes.

You always say that dreams don't mean anything. But I think this one does. I really think this dream means something.

Drip.

The monitor on the IV stand beeps, which means that the nurse needs to check vitals. I look up at the fluid bags and they're both nearly empty; I must have slept for at least forty-five minutes. I try to shake the dream from my head with a physical movement of my neck; I check my hands, clean except for a small trickle of blood that runs down from the injection site. A bruise is already forming, dark and purple, in a shape that could almost be a moth with its wings spread. The blood trickle has never happened before and I think I must have tried to tug the needle out of my hand while I was sleeping, but thankfully, the tape held the needle in place.

"Let's get you checked up and out of here," Cait says. Pippa, the older woman, is not in the seat next to mine anymore; sometimes her blood pressure isn't high enough for her infusion—today must have been one of those days. There is another man I see here quite often. His blood is so thin that he bleeds and bleeds and the nurses won't let him leave until the bleeding stops. But sometimes it seems like it never will. The nurse puts the blood pressure cuff on my arm, the thermometer in my ear, and the heart rate monitor back onto my fingertip. As the pressure tightens around my arm, I'm reminded of the particular discomfort of knowing that blood courses through my veins and moves through my body—I feel nauseous again. I've never understood how Hollie could work with bodies and all of their fluids.

"You're looking good," she says. "Let's get this taken out."

Cait pulls the clear tape away from the injection site, taking all of the infinitesimally small hairs away with it. She has gauze at the ready and I feel the needle and that small, straw-like tube as it slides out of a vein and out of my skin. I bite my lower lip—sometimes, the needle coming out is almost as bad as the needle going in.

"Hold this," she places my left hand over her right so that I can hold the gauze against the injection site before she places a piece of masking tape on top. "You're all done—make sure you watch out for anaphylaxis." I have never known anyone to smile so widely while saying *anaphylaxis*. The other nurses usually offer juice or a granola bar, but not this one. I grab my bag from the floor, stand up slowly so that I don't get dizzy and head for the exit, but something on the TV screen catches my eye. A news anchor in a plaid suit jacket with both hands on the table in front of him and a furrowed crease between his eyebrows.

The ticker tape reads: *Children at a local elementary school have been sent home with flu-like symptoms.*

He speaks: "A handful of children fell ill on their way to school and by the time the lunch bell rang, the parents of thirty-five children were called for pickups. We have our resident health expert here with more." The camera switches to a young woman in a pink blazer standing outside of a brick building that I assume is the school in question.

"Thank you, Dan. This school has been hit unusually hard and early with seasonal flu this year. It's only the first week back at school and flu season normally hits between November and March. For concerned parents who are watching, there is no need to panic. There is no indication that this is any worse than a typical tummy bug. Keep your kids home from school if they feel unwell, give them lots of fluids, wash your hands, and they'll be back to school within the week. It only takes a few germs to get a whole classroom of kids sick. Be cautious parents, but please don't panic."

The screen switches back to the man in the plaid jacket.

"Thank you, Cindy. After this brief sponsored break…"

I look back at Cait, who is busily trying to find a vein on another patient. I turn around and leave the clinic. It isn't until I get to the elevator that I think about what was on the news and something forms in my stomach, solid as a cherry pit. I call a cab, because I know you aren't coming, and I pray that it arrives quickly. I don't want to be here any longer than I need to be. When I look down, the robin is gone. There is no obvious trace that it was ever there. I want to ask you: what does it mean when the universe gives you an omen and immediately takes it away? Is it a zero-sum situation? Is it worse? I crouch down to inspect the grass and find a fragment of a blue egg nestled between blades of grass. It looks like a piece of pottery, some kind of blue ceramic; you and I will not be getting married; this will not be my something blue.

When the taxi arrives, I slide into the back seat, look up to tell the driver my home address, and I am taken aback when I see that his face is covered with a fabric mask. My dreams have been so surreal lately that I wonder for a moment if I'm still sleeping, propped up in my chair in the clinic. I snap a hair elastic against my inner wrist to make sure I'm awake and the immediate sting tells me that I am.

"Where to, Miss?"

I tell him the address and he must be able to feel me sizing him up, wondering if this is a new fashion trend or if I've gotten into a cab with a serial killer.

"I hope you don't mind the mask," he says. "Head office has told us to be careful with this bug that's going around. They say that they won't pay for sick leave if we get ill, so we need to try our best not to get sick."

"I don't mind at all," I say, "I just didn't know the bug was that bad. From what I've heard, it's just like the regular flu."

"We don't know what's coming, Miss. And if you don't mind me saying, considering that you just came out of that clinic, you'd best be extra careful."

So, now that we've established that the taxi driver cares about my well-being, we need to have a conversation about you and me.

Drip.

I call you and it goes to voicemail. I don't leave a message. As the driver turns his head to do a shoulder check, I see a blue bruise on the back of his neck where a tensed vein pulses.

I get home and you aren't there. I make a fresh pot of coffee, carefully measuring out my tablespoons, making them perfectly level. I remember reading T.S. Eliot in school and remembering that I never wanted to measure my life in coffee spoons. I wanted to have more to show for my life than kitchenware.

I take the sheets from the bed, put them in the washing machine and sit on the floor in front of it, watching them tumble and turn in the water with the vibrations pulsing through the floor. The detergent has a blue tinge—it looks like an ocean is in the drum of our washing machine. When the machine beeps and I take the sheets out to put them in the dryer, they drip on the floor, but all traces of blood are gone. This is important for you to remember. After tonight, you'll never speak to me again, but you need to remember that the blood was gone before you got home. I did everything I could to keep you from seeing it again.

Now, you are home and you have decided you're going to speak to me about our situation; you say you're going to start this conversation and set ground rules so that we don't get derailed.

You seem to be under the impression that the tracks are solid, your train car is going in a straight line, and we would have continued in a straight line if it weren't for my inability to steer. I don't think that was ever the case. You stand up to get more coffee; we're going to talk for a while.

"I'm just trying to understand," you say. "I thought you would have talked to me about this before making a decision."

"We had an agreement," I say. "We talked about this before."

"We never finished that conversation," you say. "We only ever spoke in hypotheticals."

"What else were we supposed to speak in?" I ask. "Everything is a hypothetical situation."

"Don't get philosophical on me, Willow. Not when I'm trying to understand how you could do this to me."

This makes me pause, but not for the reason you might think. If either of us is being philosophical, it's you. I don't believe that a hypothetical scenario is all that different from the real thing. It's just that one comes first and the other comes after. I remember something I had scribbled, months ago, on a hospital napkin after coming out of sedation: *we trust that softening steroids might save blood cells but the body is a candy wrapper and the mind is a wicker basket.* My candy wrapper of a body would collapse under the weight of a pregnancy. When I turned the stick over and saw those blue lines developing in the window, I felt every inch of my body settle into the floor. I felt my antibodies rile. I felt the wicker basket of my mind unraveling. You know this. You knew how this would be; you know how hard I've worked to get as well as I can. I didn't tell you because I didn't want to watch the machinations of your mind. I didn't want to see the moment when you would choose the hypothetical over everything else. Over me. I knew exactly what would happen.

Instead of speaking these thoughts aloud, I begin to make a list in my head of things that are blue:
bluebells,
peacocks,
forget-me-nots,
Blue Morpha butterflies,
gas fire,
hydrangeas,
the sky,
the ocean,
my veins,
my irises,
my chipped nail polish,
a pregnancy test.

I read somewhere that the human body cannot metabolize blue. We can metabolize red and yellow perfectly fine, but blue eludes us. Maybe it's too much for our organs to handle. Maybe the body senses blue, recognizes it in some way, and knows not to let it in.

A robin lands on the windowsill and she is large enough that I wonder if she is carrying blue eggs. I want to know how her hollow bones can stand that kind of weight.

Cherry Pit

HOLLIE WAS SIX YEARS OLD the first time she felt something die. A sparrow had collided with the kitchen window while her grandmother washed congealed pasta from blue plastic plates. When Hollie heard the crack, she knew the impact was fatal. Her grandmother helped Hollie tie her boots and button her coat—the two of them went outside to find the creature. It was so small that it took a few moments to find the body in the snow, nestled deep into a crater, plunged through the crust of ice on the surface. Hollie had forgotten to put on her mittens. She felt cold nipping at her fingertips but she wanted to see the bird. She wouldn't go back inside until after she had seen it.

"Here we are," said Hollie's grandmother who kneeled down, covering the knees of her pants in wet snow, as she plunged a hand in the icy cavity to retrieve the body. "Here, take one of my mittens." Her grandmother removed her left mitten, which was far too large for Hollie's hand, and transferred the little body into her granddaughter's cloth covered palm. The bird didn't move and Hollie thought there was something fundamentally wrong about the way its neck shifted. It was too loose—the sight reminded Hollie of her bike chains when they fell from the frame. Hollie took her other hand and placed it against the bird's chest. She felt a tiny beat, and another, and another, and then nothing. It was only when she held the bird that she realized the force of a blow did not mean immediate death. The feathers were moist and more delicate than anything Hollie had felt before. The beak was smaller than one of her grandmother's thimbles and Hollie was amazed that those legs, so ropy and lean, could ever have held any of its body weight. As though reading her mind, her grandmother said, "Birds have hollow bones, you know. They need hollow bones to be able to fly so far." Hollie kept a finger pressed against the bird's chest, just in case there was another heartbeat—she wouldn't want to miss it. Hollie's parents had died earlier that year and she would have given anything to feel their hearts beat with her head resting on her father's chest or falling asleep with her mother on the couch. When Hollie and her grandmother were in the backyard with the bird, Hollie's baby sister, Willow, was asleep in a crib. She would have no memory of their parents or any part of those first few years without them. It was only Hollie and her grandmother that would carry those memories and that sadness like baby birds in their hands.

◂◂◂◂◂

Hollie put down her razor. She was shaving the body in preparation for the man's funeral; he had died with some five o'clock shadow.

The dead deserve to look their finest; especially now.

Her mentor had reminded her of that on numerous occasions. Hollie felt at ease with the dead; unlike the living, they didn't require conversation and she rarely provided it; they didn't judge; they didn't cough without doing so into their elbows; they didn't blink too slowly or hold eye contact when they sipped from a cup. Hollie had many complaints about the human race, and she mitigated these by spending her time with the dead. She knew that no matter what, her line of work would always be in demand and her customers would always be easy going.

Hollie had heard the theories that those who have early exposure to death as children are especially suited to this kind of work. She can acknowledge that she proves the rule, but she doesn't think that her parents' deaths alone were what sent her into funeral work. It was the bird. It was those last few seconds of its heart beating and all of the moments that came after. It was putting the body in a pillowcase in a shoe box with dried lavender and rose petals. It was burying that box in the garden with one of her stuffed toys so the bird wouldn't be alone. She also remembered the moments after her parents' funeral when the director took her aside. He wasn't shocked when Hollie asked what he'd done to her parents to make them look like they were just sleeping and not dead. He answered her questions simply and clearly and didn't try to convince her to think happier thoughts.

Her client is an older gentleman, late seventies by his paperwork. Still slightly cold from the refrigeration, blue shaving cream dribbling down his face and into his ears. He was seventy-nine years old at the time of his death—he would never be older than seventy-nine. He had salt and pepper hair and a few cowlicks that she hadn't managed to flatten. She always washed their hair and used gentle shampoo and conditioner so that they'd look fresh and clean in their caskets. Hollie washed their hair, even if it was a closed casket without a family viewing or a cremation. This was one of the last times someone would take care of them; Hollie didn't want to take any shortcuts. She took a washcloth and dampened his hair before rubbing her hands into his scalp with shampoo and then conditioner. She washed their hair directly after the embalming. She thought about her sister, Willow, who was undergoing a similar process, albeit not the same, and she hoped that Willow was doing all right. She'd gotten the 'all clear,' but Willow had mentioned some difficulties. She was thankful that in her line of work, she could take as many tries as she needed. There was no squirming, no tears, and no discomfort.

Hollie worked with a photograph of the man on the table beside his head. When it came time to apply concealer and powder, she wanted him to look as natural as possible. Sleeping, not dead.

She couldn't help but notice the bruises on his arm, none of which were noted in his file. Blood always pools when a body has been laid in a specific position for a length of time, but these bruises were on the tops of his arms. She supposed there could be tissue damage of some kind, but she had no reference point. She'd never seen anything like this. There was no way the blood could have pooled in an upward direction when he had been lying on his back for days. The bruises were deep blue like a darkened sky.

She pressed one of the bruises by his upper arm with her pointer finger and she expected the flesh to bounce back the way it would if she touched a bruise on her own leg. Instead, her gloved finger went straight through as though the skin had no more resistance than a damp piece of paper. The crater swallowed her finger. There was no blood left in the body, so nothing was pouring out of the hole—she'd already done the embalming—but the skin should have held up to basic stress.

Hollie's phone beeped from across the room.

After Hollie touched the bruise on the corpse, she washed her hands five times. She knew that gloves protected her from whatever her fingers had touched. She knew she'd touched far worse and far more gruesome in her line of work. But something about this unnerved her. Unless there was some underlying condition that she didn't know about, the skin should never have deteriorated that quickly and so substantially. The room where she worked was kept between two and four degrees, but before the bodies were rolled out to her, they were kept at temperatures well below zero—enough to keep them stiff but not enough to freeze them solid. She would leave a note on his file to further investigate the bruises.

The man's eyes weren't shut and they weren't going to shut without her assistance. As difficult as it is, her first recommendation when people pre-emptively ask *what should I do with a body?* is to close their eyes. If their eyes are shut within the first thirty minutes after death, the lids might stay closed on their own even though the eyeballs will begin to sink. If not, Hollie will need to use eye caps. In Victorian times, silver coins were placed over the eyelids of the deceased to keep them shut. Hollie knew that it was impossible to look at the past without the present as a reference point, but she was fascinated by Victorian mourning traditions while others were often horrified. She remembered telling her grandmother that families routinely posed for photos with their dead loved ones. Her grandmother didn't find the practice fascinating, but Hollie could understand why families might do it. It was their last opportunity to be together in this life. She'd read that if they couldn't get the eyes to stay open or if the eyes were already deflating, they would paint open eyes onto the closed eyelids for the sake of the portrait. They also made jewelry out of hair, had picnics in graveyards, and stopped all of the clocks in a house at the moment of a loved one's death. They carried their dead outside feet first so that they wouldn't see the house they'd died in and return to haunt it. Certain communities practiced plague weddings—a marrying off of two people who had been deemed ineligible for any number of reasons: disabled, disfigured, etc. The ceremony would take place in a graveyard surrounded by the dead in the hopes that God would see them as faithful, charitable people and spare them from imminent death and destitution. Hollie had read all of this because she wanted to know where her profession had been and where it was going.

Hollie wasn't superstitious (she couldn't afford to be in her line of work), but she was enthralled by the history of her profession. Those in Victorian times would have been horrified to see her standing over the body with her tubes, eye caps, and a scalpel. They would have tied a scarf around the deceased's head to keep the jaw from dropping into a scream-like stare; she, on the other hand, sewed their jaws and lips shut with wire. She wasn't bothered by the blood or gore or the procedures she needed to perform to get a body ready for viewing and burial. But the time when Hollie was at her calmest was when she was washing their hair.

It reminded her of washing her grandmother's hair near the end when she'd been too weak to do it herself. Hollie would massage her scalp and rub coconut oil into her hair.

You've always had a soft touch, my girl.

Ever since her grandmother had died, Hollie had been hearing her voice. She hadn't told Willow, she didn't want to worry her, and she hoped that this was just a natural part of the grieving process. As much as she wanted it to end, she couldn't imagine a day when she didn't hear her grandmother's voice. She'd bought a book on the grief cycle, but ultimately, she used it as a coaster on the coffee table.

You missed a spot when you were shaving him.

"I know," Hollie said, "I just noticed that."

You did a great job on his lips, though. They look perfectly kissable.

"The wiring was easy this time, everything just fell into place."

He was a rather handsome man, wasn't he? He's just my type.

"Well, now that he's dead, maybe you two can finally be together."

"Who are you talking to?" Janelle, the secretary, popped her head into the room.

"No one. Just myself, I guess." Hollie pulled the sheet up a little higher over the man to cover his bruises. After she did it, she wasn't sure why she felt the need to keep it secret. There was nothing shameful about the body, but she felt uneasy and she bit the inside of her lower lip to keep from showing it.

"Okay, well, I'm taking my lunch break. I've left the paperwork for the Hunter file on your desk—I just need you to sign and date it and then they're good to go for the cremation this afternoon."

"Sounds good. I'll just finish up here and sign it before I take lunch."

Janelle nodded and turned around. She didn't like looking at the bodies and it made Hollie wonder how the girl had ended up here. There were other secretarial positions that would be far less distressing for her. Hollie knew that this work was not for everyone. When her grandmother had been alive, she couldn't stand to hear Hollie speak about her work or what she'd done that day. It was especially surprising to Hollie that she only heard her grandmother's voice when she was at the mortuary. If her grandmother were going to appear to her anywhere, why would it be a place she had never set foot in until the day she was rolled in on a cart? Although Hollie supposed that it also made sense. She was most prepared to see her here. It was the last place she'd seen her grandmother and it was a place for bodies and ghosts—it was definitely not a place for the living.

You should be careful dear, her grandmother whispered in her ear, *something big is coming.*

<hr>

When Hollie was seven, she swallowed a cherry pit at a church picnic; she'd meant to suck the meat of the cherry away from the pit and munch it with her teeth until it was smooth, but she inhaled and swallowed at the wrong moment. Before she knew it, the pit was travelling downward and all that was left to do was wait for a cherry tree to burst forth from her stomach.

That day at the picnic she barely left her grandmother's side, but she didn't tell her about the cherry pit. Her grandmother spoke to other people from the church that had brought watery potato salad and hot dogs that shriveled and split when they had been on the barbecue too long. She overheard an older woman pointing at a new couple, two people Hollie had never seen before, and she assumed they must be new members of the church. Hollie hated strangers, but her grandmother dragged her over and they introduced themselves. Mr. and Mrs. Baxter, the new couple, came from Edmonton. They'd moved to Calgary to be closer to their grandson who was about the same age as Hollie. Hollie could barely listen because she could feel the cherry pit rooting itself to her insides, spreading its cyanide roots into the lining of her body. She didn't want to tell her grandmother because she didn't want her to worry until she absolutely had to. If Hollie *was* dying, she wasn't going to spend her last days with her grandmother crying over her bed.

Hollie actually liked the Baxter couple. The man pulled a wrapped candy out of his jacket pocket and handed it to Hollie, and the woman had curls that were tight like bed springs. When her grandmother mentioned the couple to one of the elders at the picnic, the man bristled and said, "They probably just joined for the free funeral." Hollie couldn't understand why anyone would come to a picnic to get a free funeral.

At only seven years old, Hollie had been planning her own funeral for a few months. She would have daisies everywhere, it wouldn't be in a church, and she didn't want her grandmother to deliver the eulogy. She wanted to record it herself and play it for the attendees—let them hear her voice one last time. She'd attended the funeral for her parents, but her memories of the day were more like scenes she'd seen in a movie. She wasn't even sure that she had actually been there, she only had flashes of memory and comprehension. She remembered a room full of people she didn't know. She missed the warmth of her mother's hand and the small cloud of her father's cologne that released when he picked her up. Being fed apple slice after apple slice by her grandmother. In hindsight, it was probably to keep her mouth full so that she couldn't cry. Being placed on strangers' laps and when she wiggled to get down, they only held her tighter. She remembered a chemical smell. She remembered her baby sister crying during the ceremony, which made the funeral-goers cry harder as well. She remembered her parents looked like they were sleeping.

Now that she was an adult and worked with the dead every day, she knew the meticulous work and detail that went into making them look so peaceful. They didn't look like there'd been any kind of accident at all.

The deadness of things didn't bother Hollie. After she'd held that bird and felt the last fluttering beats of its heart, she knew she was unique. When reports of a dead squirrel had been passed through the hallways in elementary school and everyone rushed out at lunch to see it, Hollie stopped three boys from ramming a pencil through its middle the way they might skewer a marshmallow on a branch at a campfire. When she picked it up, the boys fled, perhaps fearing that she would throw it at them. She tucked the squirrel into the bottom of her backpack and brought it home. She kept it in a shoe box beneath her bed for a week before her grandmother noticed the smell.

"I don't have a problem with you bringing this home, but we need to bury them right away or put them in the freezer. I don't want you keeping this in your room."

Hollie decided to put the squirrel in the freezer so that she could take it out from time to time. She would bury it someday, but she would wait for summer when the ground wasn't frozen solid.

⚜⚜⚜⚜⚜

Hollie fiddled with the radio as she drove. She couldn't settle on any one station; they were either too static-ridden or the advertisements were too aggressively perky. She settled on a local station playing the news.

Shoppers are concerned about disruptions in production lines. Managers are urging shoppers not to panic buy and to only purchase enough emergency supplies for two weeks. We will keep our listeners updated every hour as to the progression of what scientists are calling 'Cerulean Fever.'

Hollie put on her signal and turned into the grocery store parking lot. Cerulean meant blue. The bruises flashed through Hollie's mind. She turned off the radio and left a voicemail for her sister (*call me when you can, I'm nervous about what's on the news and I want to make sure you're okay*) before leaving the car.

⚜⚜⚜⚜⚜

Hollie wrote her last will and testament the same day she swallowed the cherry pit at the picnic. She only knew the basics of the process, but she felt she knew enough to begin. She took out a notebook and a blue pen and made the following list.

I, Hollie Andrewes (age 7), upon my demise by cherry pit, give the following possessions:

- *Willow (my sister) may have all of the clothes in my closet, any drawings I have completed at the time of my death, and $5.75 (the amount of money in my ceramic owl bank)*
- *My Grandmother may have my books, jewelry, and the squirrel in the freezer. I know she will take good care of it.*

In the grocery store, Hollie took a cart so that she could buy essentials like toilet paper and a flat of bottled water. She picked up a pack of maxi pads—her grandmother had always kept a pack in the back of the car in case anyone got a nosebleed or a particularly bad cut. As she walked through the store, she noticed that some of the shelves were already empty and she realized that she'd never been able to see the back of displays before. Shelves that used to hold pasta and frozen fruit were bare. Before, there had always been ample stock. She wondered what 'after' might look like from here on out. Hollie bought supplies by circling the perimeter of the store—bread products, then dairy, then paper products, and finally produce. She picked up double of everything so she could drop supplies at Willow's apartment. It was possible her sister hadn't heard yet about the fever. She couldn't remember a time when her shopping cart had been so full. When Hollie arrived at produce, she took care to choose bananas that had at least a few days before they would ripen and apples that were crisp. A display cart full of cherries caught her eye from across the aisle, but when she picked up a handful, her fingers came away wet with mold and juice that seeped from split cherry skin. She put the cherries back down and wiped her hands on the front of her pants, but this only made it look as though she'd cut herself and had spread blood across her thighs. Hollie counted the days in her head, working backwards from payday to decide if she should split her purchase across two cards or three.

She made her way to the checkout hoping for a quick exit, but the lines wrapped around an aisle at the back of the store and halfway up another aisle. She took her place and was suddenly conscious of the nearness of other bodies. She unbuttoned her jacket, hoping to make herself feel less claustrophobic, but it didn't make a difference. There were too many bodies in one place—laughing, talking, coughing, clearing their throats. She longed for the silence and cleanliness of her procedure room.

"It's pretty wild, isn't it?"

A man was standing in line behind her and Hollie had to turn to see if he was speaking to her.

"Sorry?" she said.

"Like pigs."

She nodded but said nothing because she didn't want to engage in conversation. She just wanted to get through the cash and go.

"Like pigs on their way to slaughter and they don't even know it."

Hollie looked the man over. He wore a green vest with large pockets on both sides and safety pins that pierced through the fabric on the bottom seams. The pockets of his vest were full but Hollie didn't want to know what was in them. The man's eyes bulged out behind the lenses of his glasses. He seemed to be looking around, taking everything in, running his fingers against the edge of his vest and playing with a safety pin.

"What's your plan, then?" he asked.

"I'm just trying to get my shopping done and get home." She didn't ask him about his plans because she didn't really care to hear the answer.

"I'm a lepidopterist," he said. "I work with butterflies."

"I see."

"And what do you do, if I may ask?"

"I'm a mortician." That usually shut people up for a while.

"Ah, not all that different from my line of work. I'm a lepidopterist."

"Yes, you said."

Hollie looked over his head to see what the end of the line was like. She wanted to move away from the man but she didn't want to spend any more time in the store than she needed to. If she left her place in line and went to the back, it could easily add another thirty minutes to the wait. She was really beginning to overheat. Everyone was standing too close and the lepidopterist emanated some kind of smell that reminded her of formaldehyde. She supposed he must use chemicals for preservation, but she didn't care to find out which.

The lepidopterist was about to say something else when they both turned their heads as they heard raised voices from the front of the store followed by a shriek. Hollie caught the word *ambulance* in the clatter of voices, but she was too far away to see what was happening.

A voice came over the PA system. *There is an emergency at register seven. Please stay where you are.*

The message over the loudspeaker repeated, but the spaces between the words got smaller and smaller as the speaker picked up their pace.

"A woman collapsed by the cash register" someone from the front shouted down the line.

"What's happened?" Someone toward the back.

There is an emergency at register seven. Please stay where you are.

"Someone collapsed at the front. Pass it on."

When the message arrived at Hollie, she felt like she was in school again with the teacher starting a message with one student at the front of the line and by the time it reached the back of the line, the message was completely different.

"Someone died at the front of the store," was the message the last few shoppers received.

There is an emergency at register seven. Please stay where you are.

Shoppers were dropping their items and leaving the store, pushing their way through automatic doors that were not meant to open and close fast enough for this number of people. She worried that someone might get crushed between the mass of bodies and the glass doors. Or under foot. When the store began to clear a little more, Hollie could finally see toward the front. She saw a young woman in a sky-blue dress and stacked heels. Hollie actually had the same pair but they gave her blisters on the side of her big toe so she never wore them. The front of the sky-blue dress was covered in blood which had gushed from the young woman's nose like a stream.

There is an emergency at register seven. Please stay where you are.

Finally, Hollie heard a siren and saw flashing lights through the automatic doors. Two paramedics arrived at the woman's side and immediately began checking vitals. It took her a moment of watching to realize that the woman had blue bruises on her arm and that Hollie was standing alone, watching the paramedics load the young woman onto a stretcher. She wondered how long she'd been standing there, staring. The others had either moved to a different register or had left their items on the floor when they fled. There was no sign of the lepidopterist except for a safety pin on the floor which must have dropped from his vest.

Hollie looked over her shoulder, expecting to see more packs of macaroni and cheese spread out on the floor, but instead, at the end of the frozen aisle, Hollie saw her grandmother. It was the first time she had seen her and not just heard her voice. Hollie waved, but her grandmother didn't wave back. Hollie began to move toward her, but the closer she got, the more transparent her grandmother became. Her skin sagged off her face, her eyes were blackened holes, and her mouth was open wide as though in a perpetual scream. Hollie stopped and stared and even though her grandmother was at least twenty feet away, she heard her voice as though she was standing right behind her.

Go, she said. *Go now.*

Mourning Cloak

In the lepidopterist's study there are shadow boxes, jars of isopropyl alcohol, cotton pads, and pins. He pinches a butterfly's thorax between his thumb and forefinger, the perfect amount of pressure so that he will not crush the butterfly. He will only end its life. He has a rotation of projects so he is never without work; while one specimen is relaxing in a jar with antiseptic for a few days, he is mounting another with pins through the thorax, then the forewings, hindwings, and antennae. He knows lepidopterists who mount their specimens as though they are in flight, but he has always found this to be disingenuous. Why preserve a butterfly as though it were still alive and capable of flight when you took the care to kill and preserve it? He mounts his butterflies, flattened out on his board with wings spread wide. Some go into the shadow boxes which he lines with moth balls, ironically, to keep beetles and other pests from feeding on the specimens.

He remembers the first time he killed a butterfly—he was only a boy and he did not know the delicacy of their wings or the lightness of their bodies. He had tried to catch one in his hands when it landed on a tree. He did catch the butterfly, but its wings and antennae were bent and its body fluttered lightly, but frantically in his hands. The feeling reminded him of his mother's eyelashes when she used to bat them against his cheek until he laughed. Now, the lepidopterist shakes away thoughts of his mother, thoughts of the butterfly which he'd left to die on the side of the road. He pushes them away and pushes a pin through another thorax.

He has heard the reports of what is happening outside his studio. He was there when the young woman collapsed in the grocery store; he has heard about the hideous bruises that develop on the bodies of the afflicted, the overrun morgues, the parties people refuse to stop attending. He has heard it all and has decided to stay inside for the time being. He made one final trip for supplies (which was far less eventful than the first) and is locking himself in. He has his specimens and his work which will see him through the darkest of times. He knows it will. He straightens the photo of his mother on his workbench.

II

The lepidopterist purchased this house with his inheritance after his mother died. The money was held in trust with other relatives until he turned eighteen. He moved into the house two weeks after his eighteenth birthday and nine years to the day after her death. It is a house where children used to live. He knows because he occasionally hears the floor creak beneath his feet and when he lifts a loose floorboard, he finds candy wrappers and wind-up airplanes. He figures some child must have hidden and forgotten about them. Only this week he found a painting of a small girl with a blue face. He left these treasures where he found them; somehow it didn't seem right to move them.

On his mounting board, he has two hundred and seven different types of butterflies: Comma (*polygonia c-album*) Gatekeeper (*pyronia tithonus*) Marbled White (*melanargia galathea*), Painted Lady (*vanessa cardui*). He reads the scientific names of butterflies like poetry; they tumble off his tongue and make his breath catch in his throat the way a perfect sentence might. He organizes the mounting of his specimens by colour gradient, ranging from the Cabbage White (*pieris rapae*) to the Black Swallowtail (*papilio polyxenes*) and every colour in between except for one. He has never managed to catch a blue butterfly. He has spotted the Holly Blue (*Celastrina argiolus*) and the Common Blue (*Polyommatus icarus*), but he has never succeeded in catching one. He wonders if the painting of the blue girl could be an omen, some kind of sign that a blue butterfly is coming his way. But he doesn't believe in omens or luck, good or bad. He believes in meticulous detail; he believes in his work.

III

The lepidopterist is about to begin the delicate process of transferring the newly dead butterfly to a jar with a cotton pad soaked in antiseptic solution. The butterfly will stay in the jar for a few days and when he removes it, the wings and body parts will be as malleable as when the butterfly was alive. He caught a Mourning Cloak (*nymphalis antiopa*) and pressed the thorax as usual. He needs to get the butterfly into the jar and seal it before the body becomes too delicate to handle. He is about to lift the butterfly when the doorbell rings—he berates himself for not having drilled a hole through the doorbell wires when he first moved in. The lepidopterist does not plan to open the door at the best of times, and with this new fever going around, he has no intentions of entertaining a stranger. He lifts the butterfly again, as gently as he can, remembering a baby bird that had flown into a classroom window when he was a boy. The teacher told them to ignore it, she would call the caretaker to deal with the body, but he could not focus until he had seen the bird. He got a hall pass to use the bathroom and left the school building through the back door closest to where the bird hit. When he got to the window, he thought there was nothing there, but when he looked harder, he found a finch in the grass, opening and closing its beak in slow motion. Its neck was at an odd angle, bent slightly, in a way he knew meant imminent death. He picked up the bird, so much lighter than he'd expected, and gently squeezed its throat until its mouth stopped moving. He returned to class with the bird's body tucked into the pocket of his uniform pants and transferred it to his thermal lunch kit when the teacher wasn't looking. When the other students went out to look for the bird at recess, they found only a few loose feathers nestled in the grass.

"Something must have come and eaten it already," said one boy.

"Don't be such a dummy," said another, "the caretaker probably already came and got it."

"What if we just imagined it?"

"What? All of us imagined it at the same time? That's the stupidest thing I've ever heard."

His first secret was tucked into his lunch kit between a pudding cup and an apple. Upon returning home, he put the bird into a jar with rubbing alcohol, hoping that the fluid might preserve the bird in its current state. He wanted to keep his secret safe forever. He checked on the bird each day, but it wasn't preserving in the flawless way he'd hoped. The feathers were separating from the body—some floated to the top and others sank—and the bird did not look as it was supposed to. With the feathers lifting, he could see skin, the kind of grey that reminded him of smokestacks he'd seen in the country. He took the jar with the bird and the alcohol and emptied it into the wooded area behind the house. When he went back a few days later, any hint of the bird was gone.

The doorbell rings again. He puts the Mourning Cloak back down on the table and ventures upstairs, not to open the door, just to see who is so insistent on bothering him and his work. The intruder seems to have given up on the doorbell and is knocking on the door instead. These are steady, calculated knocks, like a metronome. The lepidopterist feels each one in the back of his skull. He waits until the noise stops and then goes to the peephole. When he looks through the small piece of glass, no one is there. He sees only an unoccupied front step.

They must have given up he thinks to himself. He returns to his work on the Mourning Cloak.

IV

The lepidopterist is eating instant oatmeal for lunch. His work on the Mourning Cloak is done for at least a few days. He eats oatmeal and listens to the radio.

His life isn't all that different from before the fever—he had never been particularly social and that was fine by him—now he just had a good reason to stay in that no one could question. His neighbours had stopped inviting him to their 'end of summer' barbecue get-togethers and birthday parties and Thanksgiving celebrations. There was a small part of him that did mind when the invitations stopped coming. He wouldn't attend and they knew he wouldn't, but he couldn't deny the part of him that still wanted to be invited. *Anyway,* he thinks, *just as well that I'm home with my work.*

He turns off the radio. When his oatmeal has cooled enough to eat, he drizzles liquid honey over the top, and then brown sugar. The top of his oatmeal is crisp like his mother used to make. He has only gotten two spoonfuls into his mouth when he sees something out of the corner of his eye. Something blue floating by the window. Was it a trick of the light? Or could it finally be the blue butterfly he'd been chasing all these years? He leaves his oatmeal on the counter, runs downstairs to get his net and trap, and fastens his wraparound sunglasses around the back of his head. He will need impeccable focus to catch this butterfly. Within a minute, he is outside, standing as still as he can by his front door so that he can catch every possible movement around him. Out of the corner of his eye, he sees a flash of blue rounding the corner to the back of the house. He rounds the corner, crunching through the detritus of dead leaves and fallen branches, and can see it in the distance, only about ten meters away. He just has to wait for the butterfly to land somewhere, then he can creep up, quietly, and drop the net before it can fly away. He still can't believe his luck at finally seeing the blue butterfly. He's never seen one in Alberta before and the only reason he'd stayed in the kitchen to eat his oatmeal was because he was listening to the horrors on the radio. And now, he is finally going to catch it. *Funny*, he thinks, *how things work out.*

V

The butterfly slows slightly and lowers down onto a stock of creeping bell flower that had sprung through the soil in the side garden. The flower is noxious and pervasive—the lepidopterist worried it might work its way through the foundations of the house and into his studio in the basement. He'd read that the root systems of the plants spread wide like human nerves branching out from the heart. He would have to do something about the weeds. As the butterfly lands, the lepidopterist readies his net which is long and translucent. He is two feet away from the butterfly and inching closer and closer until he can confidently lower the net and know the butterfly will not have time or room to escape. He is finally close enough; he raises his net to the appropriate height and lowers it as quickly as he can. He has it.

"Sir?"

The lepidopterist turns around and finds a young girl, probably nine or ten, holding a rabbit in her arms. It takes him only a few moments to realize that the rabbit is dead and has been for some time—long enough that rigor has set in, but not long enough that the eyes have begun to deflate. The rabbit is still flopped over in her arms as though it is a well-loved toy.

"What do you want?" he asks her. He holds the opening of

his butterfly net shut because the child has interrupted his usual process. "I'm very busy, what do you want?"

"I heard you could fix things," she says. He wonders where she might have heard such a thing. He supposes that his neighbours might have been talking about him and his work and one of their children might have overheard.

"What kinds of things?" he asks.

She holds the rabbit a little higher. "Like this. You could make this rabbit alive again."

"No one can do that."

"They said you could."

"Who is *they*?" He is getting more and more suspicious. He looks behind him to see if other children might be nearby, if this is some kind of trick. He doesn't see anyone but that doesn't mean that there isn't a horde of children ready to run out at him as soon as his back is turned.

VI

When he was young and his mother was ill and in hospital, his Uncle Ivan had visited for the first time. He'd gone to a Halloween party at his uncle's insistence. *You need to be around normal children, otherwise you'll be like you are for the rest of your life.* Uncle Ivan had only come to visit for the first time when his mother became too ill to stay home. His mother never spoke to him like that. She knew he was different, quiet, a little odd, and she said she loved him for it. *My little scientist,* she used to call him. Uncle Ivan didn't try to hide his disgust at his nephew's specimens and experiments. In order to appease his uncle, he agreed to go to the party even though he hadn't received an invitation. He didn't have a costume prepared, so his uncle pulled an old sheet from the closet, cut holes for eyes, and draped it over his nephew. When the lepidopterist arrived at the party, it didn't seem so terrible. He talked to a few of the kids he knew from school, the ones he knew were at least kind even if they didn't want to associate with him.

He had been at the party for twenty minutes and nothing had gone disastrously wrong; he hoped his mother would be proud when he next visited her at the hospital. The mother of the girl who was hosting the Halloween party came downstairs with more snacks; peeled grapes so that they felt like eyeballs, biscuits shaped like mummy fingers, everything slathered in red food colouring and corn syrup, congealing like blood.

"How's your mother, dear?" she asked when she saw that he wasn't diving toward the snack table headfirst like other children.

"She's in the hospital."

"I know, but hopefully she'll be home with you soon."

"She won't be. The doctors told her she's going to die soon." She didn't seem to know what to say in response and so the boy continued. "When she's gone, they're going to take her blood out of her body, fill her with chemicals, and sew her lips shut so that we can have her at the funeral."

"What a ghastly thing to think about, young man. I hope your mother doesn't hear you talk like that," she pursed her lips, "it would break her heart." She walked off and left him sitting on the couch by himself. It was only 7:00 p.m.; his uncle wouldn't be back to pick him up until eight.

He'd drunk so much punch that he desperately needed the bathroom, but he didn't want to leave his spot on the couch in case he returned to find someone else had taken it. He waited until he couldn't hold it any longer. He asked someone about the washroom and they pointed in the general direction of upstairs. He took care not to trip on his costume as he walked upstairs. After he'd finished and was washing his hands, he went to open the door, but it didn't budge. He didn't remember locking it when he'd come in, and he couldn't see how he might have locked it by accident. His breathing quickened; he heard a giggle from the other side of the door. One laugh started, another piped in and before long, he heard a chorus of laughter on the other side of the door.

"Let me out, please."

"I'm afraid we can't do that," a boy's voice, followed by a girl's voice. "You're our experiment now. We want to see how long you can last in there."

"Let me out." His chest was beginning to feel tight like someone had stretched his arms behind him until they could go no further. "Let me out, let me out." There was more laughter. Each time he spoke the laughter grew. His nose began to run as if a tap had opened and when he looked down at his hands, they were covered in the blood that was streaming from his nostrils and onto the floor, the bath rug, the edge of the sink. He tried the door again but the blood made his hands slick and he couldn't turn the handle even if it were unlocked. He sat down on the floor and refused to cry; he needed a plan. When he remembered he was still wearing the sheet as a costume, he pulled it over his head and used it to wipe up what blood he could.

He looked up and saw a small window, maybe just big enough for him to fit through if he could get it open. He closed the toilet seat lid and climbed on top to try and pry the window open. Once he'd gotten it, he clawed at the screen with his fingernails until he could rip it out completely. His fingertips were bloody, but he wasn't sure if he'd cut them on the screen or if it was residual blood from his nose bleed. He hoisted himself through the window, leaving the laughter and snickering sounds behind him. He ran to the hospital to see his mother, but when he got there, a woman in a white coat told him that she was already gone.

VII

He looks at the girl with the rabbit and feels a twinge of compassion for her, holding this dead animal, and that twinge takes him by surprise. She reminds him of himself when he was younger, slipping birds into his lunch kit. His butterfly net is still in his hands, but when he looks down, there is no blue butterfly in it.

It might have flown away when he was lowering the net and he just hadn't seen it, but he doesn't know how that is possible. The girl stands in front of him with the limp rabbit in her arms and a shiny stream of snot running down from her right nostril.

"I can't make it alive again," he says, "but I can make it look better. I can take everything out that's inside, stuff it, and give it back to you and you can keep it forever. But it won't be alive."

The girl seems to consider his proposition for a moment with a furrowing brow and her eyes slightly narrowed.

"Can I help?" she asks.

VIII

He brought her into his house—his first visitor in two decades—and pulled up a second chair in his studio so that she could watch the process. He started by measuring the rabbit's length and width, then with his skinning scissors, he pushed down to pierce the skin and slit through its middle all the way to its chin. He hadn't performed an operation like this in years and he'd forgotten how slippery his hands and tools would become as soon as he'd made the first incision. He reached below his desk for a handful of sawdust which would help to dry some of the blood. He continued to slit very gently so that he could remove the fur. Once he had the outer shell of a rabbit in his hands, he rubbed it with borax to keep the fur from rotting after being stuffed. He took extra care to clean the mouth, eyes, and nose, since the cavities were small and bacteria could flourish in tiny spaces. At one point, he turned around because the girl had been quiet for some time and he worried that the blood and cutting and gore had disgusted her, but when he looked at her out of the corner of his eye, the girl's face was blue. He blinked and she looked like herself again, smiling and curious. He still felt a stinging disappointment that he'd lost the blue butterfly. He didn't know how he could have missed it.

"Is this what they do with people when they die?"

"Not always," he said, "some people want to be cremated. That means their bodies are burnt. Other people want to be embalmed and some want neither." He smoothed fur down to cover the seam he'd made.

"What do you want?" she asked.

He paused for a moment. No one had ever asked him that before.

"I think I'd like to be cremated," he said, "I've preserved too many specimens to want that for myself." He turned around to see what effect his response might have had on the girl, but she was standing at the top of the stairs. He hadn't heard her moving at all.

"Where are you going?" he asked, but she didn't respond. She went out the door. The rabbit remained in his hands. Its fur was soft and a shade of brown that felt like the point in fall where the colours are just beginning to shift. He put the rabbit down on his work bench, took two blue glass eyes from the drawer, and finished his stitching.

IX

The lepidopterist leans back to fit all of his mounting boards in his line of sight until he finds the first butterfly he ever preserved. Of all his specimens, this is the one that matters in the end. He pulls the pin from the butterfly's thorax. It falls to the table, and the lepidopterist's nose begins to bleed as the butterfly turns to dust. When he looks down at his arms, he can already see the bluish tinge to his skin and he knows he has invited something into his house that should never have been here. The blue butterfly lands in front of him and sits on top of the rabbit he has just completed.

Fervor

There was something wrong with my mother's baby, but I didn't understand how anything could be wrong with a baby that wasn't yet born. I had slept restlessly, hearing slamming car doors and conversations in hushed tones in the place between sleeping and waking. When I finally awoke, I stretched myself out so that a hand or a foot reached each corner of my twin sized bed; I pulled a pair of socks onto my feet and felt my toenails scrape against the wool. I would have to remember to ask mother to trim my toenails after the baby was born and she could bend again. As I left my room, I felt goose bumps lifting from the uncovered space between the tops of my socks and the hem of my nightgown.

Great Aunt Frances, who lived in the guest room downstairs with her makeshift ear trumpet and a painting of the Virgin Mary, had been complaining about draftiness for years, but I liked the way the house breathed in and out and how it hid things from me. The house had a knack for hoarding bits and pieces within its walls. I would leave my hairbrush by the bathroom sink, the one with oak leaves carved into the wooden handle. As I stood in front of the mirror the next day, I would reach instinctively for my brush, but only touch empty space. The hairbrush could be found beneath my bed or in my closet or in the kitchen drawer with a box of saltines. Outside, I found pinecones tucked in between bricks, nettles between windowpanes, and pieces of Great Aunt Frances's jewelry in the bird nest that hung from the low branches of the oak tree like an aneurysm. I hoped that the new baby would find the house as thrilling as I did.

On my way to my parents' bedroom, I caught the sleeve of my nightgown on the banister and was jerked backwards. I couldn't hear either of my parents speaking, only the sound of rustling fabric. I expected to see my mother, lying in bed with her bloated belly, but instead, I found Great Aunt Frances rolling a top sheet and a mattress cover into a tight ball. A metallic smell filled my nostrils and the sheets were spattered with red. I remember noticing that Great Aunt Frances had a rosary wrapped around her wrist and that she smiled into the sheets as she rolled them. It is possible that I imagined her smiling and never really saw it.

Great Aunt Frances had fallen on ice the week before and had broken her wrists and her nose. Her forearms were covered in gauze and braces. The blackness around her eyes made me think of her as a bandit, stealing my parents' sheets and creeping around the house. Great Aunt Frances spoke too loudly and she left crumbs on the counter and water pooling around the sink. I could tell that the house disliked her. Daddy was an accountant and a little too logical; he didn't see that neither my mother nor I wanted Great Aunt Frances anywhere near us.

"Good morning, young lady. It's about time you woke up." She rolled the sheets as best she could with her wrist braces.

"Where is my mother?"

"She and your father have gone to the hospital. The baby might arrive earlier than expected." Great Aunt Frances put extra emphasis on the word *might*.

"Why didn't they wake me? I would have gone with them." At this Great Aunt Frances laughed unkindly, the sort of laughter that made my nose crinkle.

"Hospitals are not for young girls. They are for the sick and the dying." Great Aunt Frances continued to roll the sheets until no red could be seen.

"Will my mother die?" I asked, "Will the baby die?"

"Why do you always ask such morbid questions? Get dressed and then make yourself useful—and for heaven's sake, brush your hair."

"My hairbrush isn't where I left it and I haven't found it yet."

Great Aunt Frances sighed.

"I will fix you breakfast and then I'll go and see your mother and my nephew."

"May I come too?"

"Bring these sheets downstairs and fill the compartment with bleach."

Great Aunt Frances left the room without providing an answer to my question.

I walked to the top of the stairs to watch my Great Aunt's retreat. I began to imagine that my arm might extend to the soft space between her shoulder blades, I would apply just enough pressure to send my Great Aunt's top half down the stairs faster than her bottom half, and I would watch the resulting fall from the highest point in the house. Frankly, I thought, the house would be grateful if Great Aunt Frances were dead. I enjoyed the image of her saggy body at the foot of the stairs and then descended with the metallic-smelling sheets bundled in my arms.

As I passed the kitchen, I heard Great Aunt Frances muttering to herself, stirring oatmeal on the stove in time with her intonation:

Let there be none to extend mercy unto her; neither let there be any favour to her fatherless children. Let her posterity be cut off; and in the generation following let their name be blotted out. Amen.

And she began again. It is possible that she was saying something else and I misheard, but I remember noticing how her skin had lost its brightness since she'd moved into the house. Her rosacea had calmed and her cheeks held a certain pallor. None of us had been leaving the house much since the fever began. Mother was too weak and too vulnerable, Great Aunt Frances was too old, and they all worried that I was too irresponsible to avoid catching the fever if I went outside. Great Aunt Frances thought the fever was a punishment from God. He had seen our sinful ways and had decided to smite us in punishment. I didn't think that bacteria or viruses fell under God's purview, but Great Aunt Frances wouldn't hear of it. I thought about my parents going to the hospital and wondered if it wouldn't be better for the baby to be born in the house. We knew there was no fever in the house; I couldn't say the same about the hospital.

I watched my Great Aunt for a few moments, reminding myself that she was very much alive, unfortunately. I left Great Aunt Frances praying in the kitchen and went down the stairs to the basement where I dropped the sheets by my feet and pulled the string on the light bulb. The room illuminated to welcome me. My parents rarely came down to the basement and I often forgot that the basement was part of the house. I was surrounded by empty bookshelves and a china hutch filled with ancient dinner plates and teapots. I often wondered where the baby would sleep and suspected that the basement could be made comfortable and might suit the baby well. Perhaps babies were like birds and wouldn't cry under cloak of darkness. I picked up the sheets and unrolled the tightness my Great Aunt had created. The red covered more than half of the sheets and formed a butterfly shape at the centre. I picked up the bottle of bleach with two hands and was careful not to spill. Once I had emptied enough bleach, I closed the lid, flipped the switch, and felt a familiar vibration beneath my fingers. When I looked down, I saw that some of the red had seeped through the front of my nightgown.

"Julia!" Great Aunt Frances called from upstairs. I removed my nightgown and placed it in the washer with my parents' sheets. I turned out the light and climbed the steps toward the kitchen as goose bumps spread across my bare stomach. I stood in the kitchen doorway and waited for Great Aunt Frances to turn around.

"God almighty—what do you mean by this? Gallivanting about naked?"

I turned to climb the steps when Great Aunt Frances grabbed the metal spoon from the pot of oatmeal that had begun to burn on the stove and she struck my left hip with it. The gesture did not surprise me in the slightest, but the sensation of scalding oats on my hip made my breath hitch in my throat.

"You see what you made me do?" Great Aunt Frances put the spoon back in the pot where it stood up straight in the congealed oats. "The oatmeal is *black*—a bad omen if ever I saw one. Now your mother will die and my nephew will die and the baby will die. Are you happy?"

I turned and ran up the stairs. I know that my Great Aunt watched my white buttocks retreating into the safety of my room. Great Aunt Frances often told lies but had never delivered such a spotless performance. An inch or two of my hip was puckered and pink, it might even scar, I could hear her voice saying *but what did you expect? Running about naked with your mother the way she is. My nephew has done very poorly.* If she could have found a way, I'm sure Great Aunt Frances would have blamed me for Cerulean Fever as well. Clearly, God's wrath was in full response to my behaviour alone.

I was unwilling to cry in front of my Great Aunt. Once I was safely back in my room, I reached for the box under my bed where I kept salves and potions I had made from river water, honey, and plants I'd plucked from the garden in summer and had pressed between Numbers and Deuteronomy. I had begun keeping certain salves and herbs as soon as I heard my parents say that the baby was too small. I knew that I would need to be prepared to help by rubbing the baby's small heels, knees, and elbows with my salves to make it grow. I smeared the ointment over my burnt hip and selected my clothing for the day: a grey woolen skirt, a white turtleneck with lace around the cuffs, a pair of high black socks, and shoes that my mother had deemed 'too practical.' When I came back down the stairs, there was a bowl of blackened oatmeal on the table and a note written in my Great Aunt's spidery writing.

Gone to the hospital. Don't let anyone in the house. Stay out of my things.

Your Great Aunt,

Frances

When Great Aunt Frances said *stay out of my things,* I knew she meant the velvet valise case in her room. She tried to keep it secret, but she should have known that the house would never let her keep a secret from me. I prodded at the cold oatmeal with a spoon and decided that I wasn't going to eat anything my Great Aunt cooked. Even if my mother and father died and I was left with Great Aunt Frances, I wouldn't touch a bite.

I had an empty afternoon ahead of me. I thought about my mother and father and the baby and how none of them would be coming home if Great Aunt Frances was telling the truth. I decided to take the opportunity to explore the house by myself since I was rarely left alone. I walked through each room twice and took notes in my spiral bound book of what changed between rounds of the house: the placement of the curtains, how the butter knife switched from one side to the other on the kitchen counter, the number of snowy footsteps Great Aunt Frances had left in the walkway. On the second tour of the house, the footsteps were gone. I was about to begin my third tour when the doorbell chimed.

I froze. The doorbell had never rung before when I had been on my own. But, I thought, the house will take care of me as it always has. Perhaps it was my parents and they had forgotten to bring a house key in their midnight rush to the hospital. At the time, I was too small to look through the peephole, and so I opened the door blindly.

I kept the screen door shut between myself and whatever stood on my front step. When I looked up, I saw a tall woman, at least a foot taller than my mother and at least two feet taller than Great Aunt Frances. She carried a black bag at her side. The woman looked over my head as if she thought the door might have opened by itself until her gaze scanned downward and landed on me.

"Hello," the woman said.

"Hello."

"Is your mama home?"

"No, she's out."

"Is your papa home?"

"He's out too."

"Do you have any idea when they might be back?"

"I don't know," I paused, "my mother is having a baby." The muscles in the woman's face shifted, but I made no motion to open the screen door.

"A baby! How exciting for you to have a little brother or sister on the way."

"Maybe. I don't know."

"You don't know what?"

"If I'll have a brother or sister. Something is wrong with the baby."

"Oh dear," the woman said, "how awful." I hadn't thought about it being awful; it was just different from what I had expected.

"What's your name?" the woman asked.

"Julia." I had meant to pause before I said my name, but had paused after, which didn't make for a pause at all.

"Julia. It's lovely to meet you."

I nodded because the woman *was* lovely. Her cheeks were flush from the cold and she had a little mole between her eyebrows that I thought was the most beautiful thing I had ever seen. Her hair was mostly tucked under an old-fashioned hat, but I could see that it was the colour of blackberries crushed between my fingers. I noticed that the woman was shivering and kept looking over my shoulder to glance into the house.

"Say Julia, could I come in for a cup of tea? It's awfully cold out here."

I took a moment to consider. I thought of Great Aunt Frances's instructions and decided to nod and reach for the screen door handle.

"You're sure your mama won't mind? I wouldn't want you to get in trouble because of me." She spoke as she passed the threshold of the house. As the door opened and shut, I heard the girl next door singing. *Little boy blue... you got to catch it if you can...* the sound dissipated as the door closed.

"She's busy with the baby. She won't mind."

The woman placed her case on the floor in such a way that I thought it might hold fragile items.

"What a nice home you have."

"I think the house likes you," I said.

"How can you tell?"

"The house moves with you. Do you see how the curtains sway?"

She looked around her and nodded, as if the house pleased her as much as I was pleased by her.

I'd never had a guest of my own before, but I had watched my mother fill the kettle halfway, place it on the stove, and turn on the burner. I did the same.

"Thank you for letting me in. It's very kind of you." The woman took off her hat and placed it on the kitchen table. I took tea leaves and spooned them into the basket of the teapot. We sat without speaking for a few minutes. She looked around the room and over my head as though someone was standing behind me.

"Do you know why I knocked on your door today, Julia?"

"No," I paused, "why?"

"Because I had a feeling."

"What kind of feeling?"

"A feeling that something was wrong."

"How did you know?"

The kettle began to boil and shriek from the other side of the kitchen.

"I could feel it in my bones."

I took the kettle from the stove and poured water into the teapot, and then I prepared the cups and saucers.

"Do you take milk or sugar?" I had heard my mother ask this often.

"Both, thank you." As I added a sugar cube and a splash of milk to both teacups, I realized that I had never asked the woman's name. I thought she seemed like a Jeanette or a Delaney. I didn't want to ask and be disappointed by any other name.

"I could help your mother, you know," said Jeanette or Delaney as I handed her a cup of tea.

"How could you help her?" I wondered if Jeanette or Delaney had a collection of jars and containers in the bag at her feet like I had beneath my bed.

"I know people," Jeanette or Delaney began, "who can fix someone. They put their minds and their voices together in an incantation and people get better."

"Have you seen them?" I asked.

"I have. I've even joined the ritual sometimes when they need another voice. You see, my twin sister was unwell when I was your age. She had a rattling in her lungs and blood in her stomach. One day, a woman came to my door and said she thought that I needed some help. I asked if she had come for my sick sister and she said yes."

I sipped my tea, unsure what to believe. The house liked Jeanette or Delaney and my eyes were drawn to the mole again and again. In the years since, I've wondered if I imagined that mole between her eyes. It's such a singular detail.

"Like witches?" I asked.

"A little like witches. They fixed my sister within a week. The only problem," Jeanette or Delaney continued, "is that they work so hard fixing other people that they don't have anything left for themselves."

My tea was already a drinkable temperature, but I blew on it anyway, careful to position my upper lip the way my mother did.

"They can save your mother and the baby, but they need something in return."

I thought of all of my possessions.

"I have no money."

"Does your mama have any jewelry?"

"My mother doesn't wear any."

"They can't help unless they have something in return."

Great Aunt Frances, I thought. Great Aunt Frances's back was always stooped and her neck dipped under the weight of her necklaces.

"Excuse me one moment," I said the same way I'd rehearsed for the day I would have company. I left the kitchen in pursuit of the guest room where Great Aunt Frances lived. A painting of the Virgin Mary hung above the bed. Her arms were outstretched and her eyes looked as though they might roll back into her skull. The yellow background of the painting reminded me of ground mustard. In a velvet case under the bed, I found what I was looking for.

When I returned to the kitchen with the velvet valise, Jeanette or Delaney had nearly finished her tea and smiled at me as she reached for the case. She opened the lid and saw Great Aunt Frances's necklaces, rings, and trinkets. She picked out one necklace that looked like a drop of blood and held it by the chain so that it slid between her fingers like a small snake.

"These will do very nicely," she said as she took another, a gold chain with a sky-blue pendant from the valise and dangled it between her fingers. I thought that the necklace would suit Jeanette or Delaney much better than Great Aunt Frances.

"I will take this with me if that's alright. They will only start the ritual once they see what you have offered." She drank the rest of her tea in one gulp and when she placed the cup back on the table, I saw that the sugar cube had not fully dissolved. I had forgotten to stir it before handing the cup over. Jeanette or Delaney stood up, placed her hat back on her head, and walked towards the door with her own case in one hand and Great Aunt Frances' case in the other. I followed closely behind and nearly walked into her when Jeanette or Delaney stopped a few feet from the front door. She turned around and put a hand on my shoulder.

"The baby will be fine."

With that, I unlocked the door and Jeanette or Delaney went back into the snow-filled afternoon. The girl next door was no longer singing. When I closed the door behind her, I counted the number of footsteps she had left on the walkway, so that I could double check the number later.

I couldn't wait to see Great Aunt Frances's face when she reached under the bed and found her valise missing. She would look up at the painting of the Virgin Mary and then begin to search frantically. I would insist that I had spent the afternoon alone. This would be another reason she could use to blame me for the fever. I didn't mind. I sat back down at the kitchen table after putting the kettle on for a second pot of tea. The water began to boil and the phone rang just as the kettle reached the peak of its whistle. It was my father calling from the hospital to tell me that the baby was small, but alive and well, and my mother had come through the birth just fine. I sat and sipped the tea that was left in the pot I had made for Jeanette or Delaney. Mother and father arrived that evening with a fleshy bundle wrapped in blankets and tucked into a carrier. The baby's lips were the colour of strawberry juice.

We sat in the living room with the baby between us and I didn't ask where Great Aunt Frances had gone. They would tell me about the fainting, and the bleeding, and the fever later.

Someone is Dead

M

M lifts her shirt and tucks it under the band of her sports bra. She rips open the packaging of an alcohol wipe and uses it to disinfect a patch of skin a few inches to the left of her belly button. Circle left, circle right, circle left. She counts to thirty to make sure that the alcohol dries. She forgot to let it dry once and the needle carried the wet alcohol into her body with her weekly dose of biologics. It stung and she vowed never to do this again (she would take illness over the needles any day), knowing that she would be back in the bathroom, with a new needle and a new alcohol wipe in one month's time. She took the syringe from the fridge thirty minutes ago so she wouldn't have to feel freezing liquid as it entered her body. She pinches a bit of fat from her belly at the spot she'd disinfected. She breathes in. She takes the syringe between her fingers and plunges it into her belly. Once the needle is nestled into her skin, she pushes the plunger which always goes down slower than she'd like and she feels the fluid as it seeps inside her. When she did her injection three months ago, Gus had stood on the other side of the bathroom door.

"How's it going?" he asked.

"It's in," M would say. "It doesn't sting too bad this time."

The plunger is pushed almost as far down as it will go. When she pushes it that little bit more, the plunger clicks into place. When she removes her finger from the plunger, the needle retracts fast enough that she barely feels anything as it leaves her skin. She breathes out. She's hardly heard the music she painstakingly selected beforehand. Now that Gus isn't there to fill the silence, she needs something to listen to. She was tempted to search "music for self-injections" in the YouTube search bar the way she might have done for music to exercise, study, write, have sex, sleep to. A search would be fruitless, so she chose the first song that came up on shuffle.

"I'm done," M says as though Gus is still there to listen. She puts a bandage over the injection site where a bead of blood is forming. She opens the door and almost expects to see Gus standing on the other side with a fresh cup of coffee in his hands. Instead, she enters an empty doorway. Negative space, she thinks. Nothingness.

Gus has been gone for three months. In the first weeks after his departure, M had not left the bathtub except to sleep and use the toilet. Her mother came by once a day to bring sustenance and to try to convince her daughter to leave the tub. If her mother, Josephine, wasn't bringing her food, M wouldn't eat. M didn't want to go back to Gus's apartment to get her things. Her sister, Nora, had gone and collected what she needed: some clothes, her laptop, her phone charger, and a toothbrush. She wasn't going to use any of it. She was going to stay in the tub until she became part of it, and it would become a part of her. She was going to ignore everything that was happening outside, the fever, Gus, the increasing sense of panic and dread she felt radiating from her mother and sister. That could all happen outside and she would stay here beneath the warm water.

She had placed her hands on her belly beneath the water, which was more tepid than warm. It would soon be time to drain the tub and refill. She pushed slightly, a habit she'd developed when she still thought she was going to have a baby.

"Where'd you go, little bean?" she asked.

Nora

Olive stands in the kitchen doorway with her arms full of blankets in plastic wrap, canned goods, and bottled water. She has put on another pair of sweatpants and rubs her hands against her face until the apples of her cheeks are the colour of figs.

"Did you get candles?" she asks.

Nora had meant to buy candles at the store and had completely forgotten. They had been going to the grocery store every two weeks to minimize contact with the outside world. She had been at the store in the early days of the fever when a woman collapsed at the cash register and later died in hospital. Every time she left the house, she mentally prepared to see something similar.

"Shit," she says. "I'm sorry, love."

Olive turns around without a word and goes further into their house. Nora knows that when Olive is truly pissed off, she won't say anything at all. Sometimes, Nora wishes Olive would let her have it. Just as she is about to stand up and follow Olive to apologize again, the power goes out. Olive's phone beeps to let her know that it is no longer charging and the lights flicker once, then stay out until the room is enveloped in heavy silence—the kind of silence that comes quickly when all background sounds disappear. The blackness outside creeps through their windows. They don't have Wi-Fi, or a battery-powered radio and the cell towers must be down because data won't work either.

Nora keeps one hand on the wall as she searches the house for the stubs of any remaining candles, but her eyes aren't adjusting. She knows that Olive used to light a candle each night before bed (back when they had time to worry about self-care), but she doesn't know where they are kept. The candles used to make their bedroom smell like candy or burning cinnamon. Once the candle was lit, Olive would ask Nora to read to her, like a child, until she fell asleep. When reports of the fever were first surfacing, they tried to study what was coming. Nora and Olive read novels, medical journals, historical accounts, but these did nothing to assuage their fears. They had dog-eared the page of a fairy tale and underlined this phrase: *As she wrapped herself around his lungs and stomach, she whispered: You must take me everywhere. Leave no stone unturned, leave no mouth un-kissed, leave no meal untainted.* They read poetry. Ann Sexton wrote "someone is dead, even the trees know it."

After a while they stopped reading.

M

When M was a child, she'd gone to an outdoor swimming pool with her mother on weekends during the summer. There was another girl, Agatha, who would be there with her mother at the same time. Agatha and M weren't friends and they didn't plan their timing to go swimming together, but their mothers sat underneath the same striped umbrella while she and Agatha swam circles and tried to avoid speaking to each other. M didn't have anything against Agatha—she just wanted to be alone, completely isolated under the water. M could hold her breath for two lengths of the pool and wanted to be able to do three lengths by the end of the summer. Agatha usually trailed behind, dog paddling because she wasn't as strong a swimmer. After an hour or so, they got out of the water, hair full of chlorine and whatever else had been deposited into the pool and sat in front of their mothers' crossed legs to dry themselves in the sun. Agatha's mother had eyebrows like caterpillars, and she always smelled slightly like dust.

One weekend in August, M's mother had a cold, so they didn't go to the pool; when they arrived the next week, M didn't see Agatha or her mother or their red and blue striped beach towel that usually sat beside the snack shop. In fact, there were probably half as many people at the pool as usual. M wasn't sure if her mother was really friends with Agatha's mother, or if it was a relationship of convenience, like she and Agatha, but her mother asked around until she found out that Agatha was in the hospital. She'd stayed under the water too long—had swallowed masses of pool water and she'd coughed it up and vomited over the side of the pool. A teenaged lifeguard had lifted Agatha from the pool by the armpits and had rubbed her back while she coughed up everything that was inside her. Once she was finished, all seemed to be well.

A few hours later, that last bit of water she'd swallowed was still in her lungs which became inflamed until she couldn't breathe. Agatha collapsed next to the rope swing that hung from their poplar tree—her mother had seen her fall from the kitchen window. Dry drowning.

Agatha died in the hospital a few weeks later. M's mother cut an obituary from the paper to show her; the photo they had selected was a school photo with Agatha's head tilted the same way they'd posed M at her own school photos.

Nora

Nora digs in every drawer, sifting through old receipts, letters, and sympathy cards that they will never send. In the bedside table drawer, she finds a lighter and unscented pillar candles that are nearly burned down to nothing. She loads as many candles as she can into her cupped hands and props the lighter between her lips. As she leaves their room, she plans to tell Olive she is sorry for being difficult. She has barely opened her mouth when she sees Olive lying on the couch with a blanket wrapped around her shoulders.

"Olive?" A moment.

"I'm fine." Olive's voice is muffled through her elbow. The truth is that Olive feels an ache that goes deep into her spine like a small pair of scissors is working its way through her vertebrae one by one. She has never felt anything like this before and the visibility of her pain makes Nora panic.

"What if the power doesn't come back on?" Nora asks. "What if this is all part of the fever?" Sweat stains form beneath her underarms and seep through the fabric of her sweatshirt.

Olive rolls over and nestles deeper into the blankets.

"Mr. Almater next door probably tried to plug in too many things and blew something for the street. You know how forgetful he is. I'm sure everything is fine."

"You're right. I'm sure you're right," Nora says as she looks down at her feet.

They both know that she doesn't believe it.

Olive doesn't know if she believes herself. The darkness spreads so far beyond their bungalow and it is suffocating them minute-by-minute. Olive feels a slight constriction in her lungs and imagines they are full of cotton balls. And so, they wait.

M + Nora

The same week that the fever began M and Gus had hosted their engagement party at her mother's house. M was eighteen, Gus was twenty-nine; they had been dating for two hundred and seven days, and M had missed her period.

Gustav Jackson—she told Nora he prefers to be called Gus or by his last name—was a painter. She texted her sister a link to his online portfolio. One of his paintings sold for $7000 last month. Nora doesn't understand their relationship but is sure that M sees something in him. She hopes that whatever she sees will actually be there when she needs it to be. M invited Olive and Nora to Gus's most recent exhibition. He stood in the center of an empty warehouse, naked, and slowly covered his body in bright red barbecue sauce. It was reviewed in the Calgary Herald and an art critic called it "a splendiferous example of postmodern art." Nora prayed that there would be no barbecue sauce at their engagement party.

When Nora and Olive arrived at the party, it looked like they'd walked into a frat house. A banner of golden letters was stapled through the wall (*Mom will not be pleased*, thought Nora) that spelled out *SAME PENIS FOREVER!* with small bits of penis shaped confetti on the floor. The confetti was stuck in M's hair. Nora couldn't see their mother anywhere; she was either in the kitchen, or she had decided to take herself away from the party and be elsewhere for the evening.

"You're late, Nora! I didn't think you were going to make it," M yelled right into her sister's ear. The music was loud and she smelled like she had already drunk quite a lot. "You know you're going to have to give me away at the wedding. I don't think Mom is even going to be there." She leaned over to kiss Olive on the cheek and she put miniature red solo cups into their hands. Nora jiggled it and when the liquid didn't slosh over the sides of the cup, she understood that it was a Jell-O shot.

"Where *is* Mom, anyway?" Nora asked.

"Who knows? She's been against Gus and I being happy together since day one."

"Which was how many days ago?"

"Two hundred and seven days, to be exact." M downed another Jell-O shot.

"I'm going to go check her bedroom. Try not to be too tough on her, M. You're her baby and she loves you."

M was too busy throwing penis shaped confetti at Olive to hear her sister. Nora looked at Olive to make sure she was okay with being left with M and gave a small nod and kissed her fingertips before touching Nora's face.

Nora pushed her way through boys that looked like high school quarterbacks, remembering that they probably were high school quarterbacks, until she could get to her mother's room. The door was closed, but a sliver of light shone through the space underneath.

"Mom? It's me. Can I come in?"

Nora opened the door a crack and found her mother sitting cross-legged on her queen-sized bed. The floral quilt was perfectly pulled so that equal parts hung off all corners of the mattress.

"You're not going to join the festivities?" she asked her mother.

"I would rather eat penis confetti off the floor," was her response. So, she had seen the staples in her living room wall.

"It's not ideal, I'll grant you that," Nora said.

"Not ideal? You and I both know she's making the biggest mistake of her life." Josephine closed her eyes and pinched the bridge of her nose between her fingers. "She's only eighteen. How can she possibly know what she wants yet?"

Nora paused before saying, "It *is* possible that they really do love each other." Josephine pulled her knees into her chest and hugged them in tight but said nothing. "Do you want anything to eat? I can bring you something. A Jell-O shot perhaps?" Nora knew her mother would feel only marginally better if she ate something.

"I'm fine. But Nora, can you try to talk some sense into her? *Please.*"

"I'll try, but you know M. When she sets her mind to something, it's like trying to stop a bus on an icy road."

Nora left her in the room and closed the door behind her. The door clicked shut and when she turned around, Gustav Jackson was standing outside the door.

"Nora, long time no see." He leaned in for a hug, which she accepted, but not without crinkling her nose. With her face pressed into him, she noticed how the sides of his neck smelled like meat.

"How's your mother doing?"

"Fine. She's fine."

The most disconcerting part of Gus's appearance was that he had floating irises. They hardly ever seem to settle in one place, and if they did, it was as though they saw straight through all people and all things. Nora felt like he was looking through her and into the back side of her skull. His eyes were blue and cold like ocean water.

"Listen," he said, "I know I'm asking a lot of your family, and I know that this was very sudden. But Emilie is my life now. I can't imagine doing anything without her. You understand that, right?" Nora nodded, but said nothing, because she didn't understand it. She and Olive had been together for four years—they hadn't jumped into an engagement. "I'm glad we're on the same page. I think I'll need your help getting Josephine on board." She tried, and failed, to keep her left eye from twitching when he used her mother's first name, as though they were friends, and not what they actually were: people who didn't know each other beyond interactions forced by M and who had no desire to know each other. "She's very protective of you both, isn't she?"

"It's just the three of us and it has been for a long time. It's hard to change gears." He nodded at her and his blue irises floated until they focused on the painting on the wall behind her head: a print of a James Tissot called *The Dance of Death;* skeletons led a procession of people across the canvas, presumably to their deaths. Josephine always had peculiar taste in art. She'd bought a death mask of Napoleon Bonaparte at an auction a few years back.

"Anyway," he said, stretching out the beginning vowel, "we ought to get back to the party and my bride-to-be. Wouldn't want her thinking we prefer each other's company over hers."

As he snaked past to go down the hallway, Nora felt his hand tracing a slight circle at the small of her back and she smelled the meaty-ness of him again. Her skin crawled where he touched her and all she wanted to do was go home and shower for hours. As she entered the living room behind him, she locked eyes with Olive who sent a reassuring smile. At that moment, Nora wanted to leave and go home and be only with her; instead, she rested her head on Olive's shoulder when she was close enough. She smelled like campfire.

"Jell-O shot?" Olive asked, holding one out in front of her.

"Please," she took it and tried to tip it back all in one go, but the Jell-O slowly slid down the side of the cup until it reached the back of her throat. It felt like swallowing sludge, so slow that she needed to swallow a few times to get it all down. She knew she'd pay for this drink the next day, but she couldn't get through this party without at least a little bit of alcohol.

"I think I may have just been hit on by Gus," Nora finally said—the part of her back that he'd touched tingled still, not in a pleasant way, but more like sunburn when the skin begins to peel. Olive's eyes widened slightly like she wasn't even a little bit surprised.

"He's probably the kind of guy that thinks he can turn me straight or something," Nora said. Olive glanced behind her shoulder and saw him watching. She pulled Nora in with a gentle hand around the back of her neck and kissed her. Her lips tasted like red Jell-O and tequila and the feeling made something in the sides of both of their ribs tighten.

"There. Maybe he'll get the message this time."

Nora's phone buzzed in her back pocket. She didn't usually have her volume on because there was never anything urgent, but she'd put it on vibrate that night so that she would feel the alarm go off as a reminder to take her medication. The doctor had recommended taking her corticosteroids first thing in the morning since they have a stimulating effect on most patients. For Nora, however, they were as good as sedatives. They sunk her energy so low that she could hardly move without aching or wanting to cry within a few hours of taking them. In the late evening, the lows coincided with sleep, so she didn't need to feel them as much. She took the pills out of a container in her purse, a 'shopping and popping' pill carrier that Josephine had bought when Nora received her diagnosis. Both Nora and M took medication frequently, Nora took corticosteroids daily and M did self-injections of biologics once a month. Nora was born before the genetic testing craze and M was such a surprise that their mother didn't even think to try and alter her genetic makeup.

Nora slid the pill into her mouth, relegating it to the back of her tongue because it always tasted a little like copper. She downed it with a swig of water from the glass on the end table. She didn't think her doctor would advise washing her corticosteroids down with a Jell-O shot.

"Was that your glass?" Olive asked.

"Wasn't it yours? It was right by you, I just assumed you'd put it there."

Olive shook her head. "Well, that settles it, you're definitely going to get mono. You won't be able to kiss me for months and months and I'll have to find someone else to satisfy me."

With her hand on the small of Olive's back, she pulled her in and kissed her softly.

"There. Now you have mono with me. We'll be like two Victorian ladies afflicted with consumption and with nothing but each other for comfort."

"Fine by me," she said. In the corner of the room, M was gesticulating, probably explaining her hopes that Gus would make some kind of artistic centerpiece for their wedding. He, however, was looking straight at Nora with his floating eyes that didn't settle. He wasn't drinking Jell-O shots. Instead, he had a glass of what might have been scotch in a tumbler that looked like the ones Nora's father used to drink from. Nora knew the glasses were on the top shelf in the kitchen and the scotch was at the back of one of the cupboards. Apparently, Gus knew it too. He tilted his glass in her direction as though saying *cheers* from across the room and slowly nodded.

"God, what a creep," Nora said before she could stop herself.

"Do you want to get out of here?" Olive asked as she was jostled to the side by one of the teenage quarterbacks.

"Let's. We came, we saw, now let's say our goodbyes."

As they came to the corner, M stopped gesticulating and lit up.

"Everyone, this is my big sister, Nora, and her partner, Olive. Nora, this is Declan, Molly, Leah, Samuel, Caleb, Jeremy, and Noah. You've met Grace and Sophia." M pointed to each person as she said their name. Nora would never remember them all but tried to smile and at least pretend it was nice to meet them, even though she felt like they were generations younger than her—in experience if not in years. Grace and Sophia had been M's friends since childhood and would inevitably be her bridesmaids. They all stood in an uncomfortable semi-circle and smiled at one another. "You and Declan would actually have a lot to talk about—he's a poet!" Declan's eyes looked like he'd been high for months on end and Nora gave him a smile that was more a tightening of the lips than anything. The only person who caught Nora's eye for any length of time was Jeremy. The only reason he caught her attention was because of his pallor. He looked white and dewy and sweaty except for his cheeks. Two blemishes across his cheekbones that were a shocking shade of blue. *Makeup?* Thought Nora. *Or possibly some kind of condition?*

"We're going to be taking off. Thanks for having us and I hope you enjoy the rest of the party," Olive said while Nora looked at Jeremy and tried to discern what might be wrong with him. His eyes were unsettled like Gus's, but not because of floating irises. It almost seemed like his pupils might roll up and under his lids at any moment.

Nora's focus came back to the conversation. "Congratulations again to you both," she forced herself to look Gus in the eye and smile. "I think you'll be very happy together."

"Oh, Nora. That means the world to me, it really does—to know that we have your blessing," M lowered her voice and looked around to see if anyone other than Nora and Olive were listening. "There's one little thing I still need to tell you. Can you keep a secret?"

Nora nodded and M leaned in, smelling of Jell-O and tequila, and whispered *I think I might be pregnant.* It was no surprise to Nora, but she wanted to take her sister out of the room, lecture her about drinking while pregnant, or even only possibly pregnant, and then give her the biggest hug because she was desperately unprepared for everything that was about to come. Nora wanted to wrap herself around M like a protective shield and keep her from getting any older, or any more pregnant, or even any more drunk that night. But she couldn't. She leaned away as Gus took M by the elbow and guided her towards a conversation happening on the other side of the semi-circle.

"Emilie, we need you to help settle something. We were looking at that ghastly painting Josephine has on the wall and wondering how one might come across a piece of art like that. Did she see the painting before she bought it? Or did a skeleton deposit it in the night and demand it be displayed?"

"I would have to assume the latter," she said. Nora had never heard M say *latter* before. "A skeleton crept into her bedchamber and after having his way with her, he left the painting as a reminder of her mortality. That's why she's so damn miserable and mean all the time."

The crowd gathered around M began to laugh and hoot. Nora hadn't heard her be so cruel before, especially not to their mother, but she looked at Gus and he smiled as though she was a dog who had finally performed the right trick. If their mother was still sitting on her bed, she would have heard the whole conversation.

Nora took Olive's hand in hers and said, "Let's get home. I've had enough celebration for one night." She wondered if the baby would be born with a caul like M had been, or if it would be born screaming into bright hospital lights with a father whose eyes would never settle and a mother who was too young to know any better than to trust him.

In the days that followed the engagement party, there were twenty-two positive cases of Cerulean Fever in the city. Ten of them had come from the party. One week later, Gus got in his car to leave the city, an extra-large coffee with five sugars in the cupholder beside him. His destination was an arts commune he'd once visited when he was younger. He planned to call M to apologize for his cowardice once he got there. But he never arrived. The fever got him first.

Nora

Nora walks into the kitchen to make tea, places circular teabags in mugs, fills the kettle, and only remembers the power outage when the electric kettle won't turn on. It doesn't matter how many times the power goes out; she can't stop the impulse to reach for the light switch or the thermostat or the TV remote. When she comes back from the kitchen without tea, Olive is shivering on the couch with a second blanket draped over her shoulders; Nora hesitates before she reaches out and holds Olive's body against her own and tries to warm her. Nora feels that they have their own language of looks and movements—she runs a hand across Olive's forehead, much too hot, moving the hair from her eyes, hoping that their shared language of touch still means something. With her hand against Olive's forehead, she asks if Olive thinks she's contracted the fever. Olive responds by placing her own hand over Nora's which is beginning to sweat from the heat of Olive's forehead. *Yes,* that movement says, *I think I caught it.* Nora brings herself to Olive's eye level and kisses her on her dry lips. Even though Olive says she hasn't smoked in ten years, her lips always taste like cigarettes.

 "Did you know that there are massive spikes in birth rates nine months to the day after major power outages?" Nora asks, trying to lighten the darkness.

 Olive nestles deeper into the blankets.

 "So many accidental pregnancies," Olive says. "We couldn't get pregnant even if we were trying… Do you want to have a baby? When this is all over, I mean."

 "Let's talk about it when it's all over," Nora says. When Nora calls 911, the dispatcher tells her that an ambulance won't be there for an hour.

Nora places the leftover candles around the bathroom and along the edge of the tub. She manages to find some of Olive's favourite lavender bubble bath in the cabinet under the sink. She fills the tub with water that might just be hot enough and empties half of the bubble bath into the water. The water heater usually retains enough heat for a lukewarm bath. Olive looks like she is asleep. Her lips are dry and almost blue. Nora picks her up and struggles under the weight of her. Even though she looks like she weighs nothing, it is as though exhaustion has made it impossible for her to stand up on her own. She somehow feels both solid and liquid, stiff and unyielding. Olive wakes to the scent of the bubble bath, offers a little smile, and tries to support some of her own body weight.

Nora helps her undress, layer-by-layer, and feels something shift in her stomach at the sight of her. Olive looks up unflinchingly, and Nora is reminded of why she picked Olive—she remembers when they first met, Olive with her fiery hair and a jean jacket covered in enamel pins. She was sitting at a café, alone, reading a book of renaissance poetry. Nora waited until she was leaving to speak to her. The first time they kissed, it was in a change room at The Bay. Olive had asked her to come in to give an opinion on a new dress; they snuck into a room while the attendant was helping someone else. Once Olive was in the dress, orange and tucked against her ribs and hips, she climbed up on the bench, beckoned Nora closer, and then she leaned down and kissed her. When Nora later asked why she'd climbed on the bench, she'd said it was so that if the attendant came by, she would only see one pair of shoes beneath the door and they wouldn't be interrupted.

Nora helps Olive sink her body into the water, caressed by bubbles and shadows from the candles. Beneath the bubbles, the dark bruises on Olive's skin disappear and she seems so much lighter. She lifts an arm from the water, reaches out and wraps a soapy hand around Nora's, dragging it down into the water with hers. Nora will wash her hair and massage her scalp. She sits on the edge of the tub and holds her hand below the surface and waits.

M

M sits on the closed toilet seat and stares at the pregnancy test in its horrible pink box. She had bought it the day of the engagement party when her period was six days late. She had never actually taken a pregnancy test—she just had a feeling. But she found spots of blood in her underwear later that night and Gus left the next day. It is three months later and her period is late again.

She opens the box, slowly pulling the glued tabs away from the cardboard. Within the box is one pregnancy test wrapped in thin plastic with a surprisingly large set of instructions. She reads them front to back, twice, to make sure she's doing this correctly. She wonders how many women have sat on toilet seats next to bathtubs and read these same instructions; all of them hoping for something—all praying for different outcomes.

She removes the plastic cap from the test, stands up to lift the toilet seat lid, holding the absorbent part of the stick beneath her. She gets some urine on her hands, but she doesn't care. Once she's held the test under for ten seconds, she puts the cap back on and places the test on the counter, horizontally. She washes her hands and waits. She counts two hundred and seventy loud drips from the leaking faucet. Once five minutes have passed, she picks up the test, reads the screen, exhales.

If it's a girl, she thinks, *I'll name her Theodora. If it's a boy, I'll name him Joseph.*

M takes her housecoat from where she'd dropped it on the tiled floor, pulls the plug from the bathtub by its chain and hangs it on a hook behind the door.

Transcription

[Begin Transcript 00:00:15]

A: What do you know about *Cerulean Fever*?

X: I'm not a scientist or anything, but I know it started with the birds.

A: Can you elaborate?

X: How do you mean?

A: Do you know what kind of birds?

X: Blue jays.

A: Do you know how the blue jays spread the fever from their populations to human populations?

X: I don't know exactly. But I heard the fever was traced to one particular flock of blue jays. Did you know that they mostly eat vegetables?

A: I didn't know that.

X: They have a reputation for raiding other birds' nests, but they don't often eat the eggs.

A: Continue.

X: What I've read is that an especially large flock was migrating. Apparently, some blue jays migrate in winter and others don't. Scientists don't know why.

A: What were the first signs of the fever like?

X: At first, it seemed like a lot of bad luck. An early flu season, poor girls collapsing in grocery stores, kids getting sick at school. That girl that keeled over at the corn maze. We thought these were all unrelated. We didn't know then.

A: Didn't know what?

X: That it was going to kill so many of us.

A: What do you remember most about the first weeks?

X: I remember cleaning. A lot.

A: Anything in particular?

X: I think I cleaned everything. The week before the announcement from the World Health Organization, I had been prescribed a new medication and it was an immunosuppressant. I thought it was really the worst possible time to be starting anything that would alter my immune system. So yes, I cleaned everything. I disinfected cans, jars, and bottles that came from outside, I cleaned my TV remote with alcohol, I cleaned my desktop computer, the arms of my glasses, my shoes. Everything.

A: But ultimately, it was your immune disorder that helped you survive Cerulean Fever, yes?

X: It was.

A: What was your first reaction when you heard the reports of Cerulean Fever?

X: At first, I spent hours reading the news, scrolling through blogs, conspiracy theories, symptoms, causes, origins, case numbers, school closures, prevention, emergency room wait times, mask availability, homemade hand sanitizer, first reports... you get the idea. I figured this was it, you know?

A: *This* was what?

X: The end, I guess. The end of everything.

A: And how did that make you feel?

X: Like shit, to be honest. I liked my life. At least, I liked it before my health went haywire, but even that was manageable. A pandemic, however, was not. Would you excuse me a moment?

[Transcript paused 00:04:22]
[Transcript resumes 00:05:37]

X: Thanks for waiting. I printed this off for you. I remember reading it during that first week and it stuck with me.

[X hands a piece of paper to A. The contents are transcribed here:

Between 1918 and 1920, influenza (La Grippe or La Pesadilla) killed somewhere between 20 and 40 million people worldwide. Literally speaking, the word influenza is derived from the Medieval Latin word Influentia *meaning to influence. While the death tolls were high, only about twenty percent of those who were infected actually died from the disease. Very few newspapers reported on the pandemic, partly out of fear of creating mass panic, but also to keep the news from interfering with the war effort. The typical victim of influenza was young and otherwise healthy. Until they weren't. I'd like to think we'd handle it better today, but I'm not so sure that we would. For all of our scientific and medical advancements, would we really handle a catastrophe any better than they did?]*

A: And what did you make of this when you first read it?

X: It reminded me of a story passed down through my family. It's about my Great Aunt. She contracted influenza in

1918 when she was just two months old and the eighth child in her family. They couldn't risk the others getting sick, so they put her in a box and left her on the front step, planning to retrieve the body in the morning and bury it. Early in the morning, a preacher was passing by when he heard a crying infant. He picked her up, knocked on the front door, and demanded a fire in the oven. They light the fire in the oven. He put the baby inside and the heat broke her fever. She lived to be ninety-three years old.

A: And the preacher?

X: He succumbed to the influenza only a few days after rescuing my Great Aunt.

A: You believe this story?

X: I have no reason not to.

A: This piece of paper you handed to me. What did you think of their question?

X: Right away, I thought, no. We wouldn't do better. This was about influenza, which is different from what we were dealing with, but the point still stands. We would still try to find someone to blame. God, the "other," capitalism, corrupt scientists, the government.

A: And you don't think there is someone to blame?

X: I think we try our best to find someone to blame. When there's no one—because shit happens—where do we go then? How are we better off?

A: Do you think your experiences with illness have had an impact on your experience of Cerulean Fever?

X: Absolutely. I'm not the disability spokesperson [X uses hands to make quotations in the air], but yes, a lot of the people I know with disabilities or chronic illnesses were just better prepared for something like this.

A: Why do you think that is?

X: I think we need to look at our understandings of disease. Let's say you travel somewhere and you eat some oysters that tasted a little funky. You get explosive diarrhea and you can't leave the hotel for four days because you're glued to the toilet. Who do you blame?

A: What a colourful picture you paint. I suppose I would blame whoever decided the oysters were acceptable and then I would blame myself because I ate them even though I had my suspicions.

X: Fair enough. And does having someone to blame change the fact that you're glued to the toilet for four days?

A: No, I suppose it doesn't.

X: Next scenario: you're going about your life like always and then one day you start to feel different. Your body hurts, your head aches, you can't eat anything, and you don't know why. It takes you between six months and five years to get a proper diagnosis, not to mention the medical indignities you need to endure first. When you finally get a diagnosis, the simplest explanation is that your body is attacking itself from the inside. The immune system is malfunctioning. Who do you blame?

A: I suppose you can't blame anyone. If the body has failed to fight off infection or disease—

X: Has the body failed? It's still living, breathing, pumping blood, turning oxygen into carbon dioxide, loving, fucking, et cetera. If this body in question has failed, then what kind of body would we consider as passing?

A: I didn't mean to ascribe any judgement on the body.

X: I understand.

A: I apologize if I have offended you.

X: I'm used to it. It's all part of the learning process.

[transcript paused 00:11:04]
[transcript resumes 00:16:08]

A: Do you mind if I ask about your health issues? You mentioned immunosuppressants.

X: What would you like to know?

A: I suppose, and I hope this doesn't offend you, but you look perfectly healthy to me. I'm wondering how it's possible to look healthy and not be.

X: I do look healthy, don't I? But if you could see through my skin, you'd think otherwise.

A: What is your treatment plan like?

X: I've tried different medications in different forms. For a while, I got medication through an IV, but that medication failed. Multiple oral medications failed as well. So now, I give myself injections every few weeks and I take immunomodulators and regular courses of corticosteroids.

A: Do you struggle with self-injections? Most people would.

X: In the beginning, yes. I fainted the first time I tried. Thankfully, I wasn't alone. Someone caught me and helped me administer it.

A: What does it feel like?

X: It feels cold, mostly. I inject it on either side of my belly button and it stings as the needle goes in. It burns a little when I push the plunger and the medication actually comes through. Then it's over.

A: And it works?

X: For now, yes, it works.

A: I'm glad to hear that. I'd like to return to something you said earlier—about how people with chronic illnesses and disabilities were more prepared for Cerulean Fever than the general population.

X: I did say that. This is a population that has experienced isolation. That has experienced not getting what they want. That have had to be cautious around people. That have had to carry hand sanitizer with them in case they touch something. That have worn masks when they leave the house because *something* out there could hurt them. As I said before, I don't speak for everyone, but from what I see, we were ready for this when no one else was.

A: Do you in any way consider your illness a gift, then?

X: I know some people do. I certainly don't. This isn't something that I celebrate. It's also something I can't avoid.

A: If I understand correctly, the majority of the people who survived Cerulean Fever were those with pre-existing conditions precisely like yours.

X: It's true. In all of society's efforts to eradicate illness, they left themselves vulnerable to this exact kind of attack. Cerulean Fever was an antibiotic resistant superbug. There have been a few of them over the years. Can I ask you something?

A: Absolutely.

X: What do you think about the language we use when we talk about illness?

A: To be honest, I haven't thought about it much. I suppose it's a privilege to not need to.

X: I suppose it is. I've been wondering about metaphors.

A: Metaphors?

X: Yes, metaphor.

A: I confess, it's been quite a while since I've thought about metaphors.

X: When we talk about illness and disease, we always fall back on combat metaphors. Military metaphors: fighting, guarding, attacking, flooding. But don't all of these just ascribe another kind of blame?

A: They do, I suppose. If the metaphor is combat, then there must be someone to fight.

X: Exactly. But here's my question: what if there is no one to fight?

A: Because the attacker is yourself?

X: Precisely. Where do these metaphors go then?

A: I guess we might need new ones.

X: I guess we might.

[transcript paused 00:21:43]

[transcript resumes 00:27:54]

X: Do you take sugar in your coffee?

A: Only a little bit, I'm trying to cut down.

X: Here you go [X hands a cup of coffee with sugar to A].
Can I tell you a story while we drink our coffee?

A: Of course.

X: We had our first snow fall this morning. When I looked
out my window, everything was white except for a few black
spots in the middle of my backyard. I didn't know what to
think at first. I put on my shoes and when I got outside, the
black spot was a dead magpie. I thought about moving it, but
then I thought a coyote might come by. They need to eat too,
so I left it.

A: What happened to the bird?

X: I didn't look out the window for a few hours. I was
tidying up before you came. But when I looked out again,
there were at least fifty magpies. They were sitting on the
fence posts, or in the trees, or on the ground. I put my boots
back on and went outside to get a better look, but it was like
they knew I was there, watching them. It didn't matter to
them at all. The sun reflected off their feathers and a slight
blue tinge came through. One would move slightly, and a
wing would appear black again. Corvids hold funerals for
their dead. Did you know that?

A: I did not know that. Why would they hold funerals?

X: They seem to gather around the body of a lifeless bird
to improve their own chances of survival. If they can figure
out what killed *this* magpie, they might be able to avoid a
similar fate. And the strangest part?

A: What?

X: They didn't make a sound. The only sound I heard out there was melting snow moving through the downspout.

A: Corvidae are fascinating animals. I don't want to take up your whole afternoon, but I do have one more question for you if you don't mind.

X: Fire away.

A: Is there anything good that came out of the Cerulean Crisis?

X: Personally, or collectively?

A: Either.

X: I don't know if I can answer that question. I'm really not too sure what to say. Are you done with your coffee cup?

A: I am.

[transcript ends 00:31:59]

The Body
(in the House)

The Fridge Light

On an A4 sized piece of paper, draw the outline
of a torso or an hourglass. Cut the mid-section
with scissors. Place the template on the tray and
cut out the curves with a serrated knife. Shave
the edges off so that it looks like a rounded body.
Take the mold mixture and use it to form the
chest area. Coat in buttercream and smooth
with a hot knife. Powder edible luster dust
and attach pieces of lace. Add molded fondant
jewelry, pearls, flowers, or anything else that will
enhance her. Look at her, then, and ask: How
many lemons did you eat today?

Two chocolate dip, one honey cruller, five vanilla with sprin-
kles, three with Pepto Bismol pink icing. Liv watches from her
apartment window and counts the number of people walking by
with doughnuts. She thinks people like doughnuts because they
can slip their thumbs through the holes. By the time the fifth
vanilla sprinkle passes, Liv's stomach is roaring. She presses her
tongue against the roof of her mouth, swallowing a mouthful of
saliva, wills her stomach to be silent. She glances at the kitchen
cupboards and the bike lock that keeps the fridge door shut. She

counts backwards from twenty. Chilled, she takes a shawl from the back of her chair and wraps it around her bare shoulders. She decides she will finish her crossword, and then unlock the fridge for a snack of cottage cheese and pineapple pieces (two spoonfuls of each). Afterwards, she'll put the lock back on the fridge, wash the dishes and start another crossword.

When she cups her hand and breathes into it, she realizes that the back of her mouth tastes like sour milk. She remembers an article she read called *how to talk to your loved ones about their bad breath.* She thought that the article was useless since it didn't actually outline any ways to start the conversation. Careful not to offend, the author advised casually offering a mint or keeping a minimum distance of two feet at all times. Liv ran out of toothpaste yesterday and she ran out of gum this morning. She digs through her purse and finds an unwrapped hard candy tucked into a pocket with an old half unwrapped tampon, some ibuprofen, and a Swiss Army Knife. When she digs in the pocket, the warmth of her fingers melts the coating on the ibuprofen. It coats her tongue as she licks the tips of her fingers. She picks hair and dust off the candy and sticks it to the inside of her cheek. After a few seconds, she feels pieces of lint and dust floating in her mouth. She scrapes her tongue against her teeth to try and catch them, but finally spits the candy into a Kleenex. She has changed the taste in her mouth, that's enough. Her cat, Prufrock, makes a chortling sound while he stretches, then saunters to his food bowl. As he eats, the smell of cat food fills the air. Liv decides she'll do five more clues in her crossword, then she'll unlock the fridge for a few minutes.

Are you paying attention? You may have one medium-sized carrot or one piece of carob as a meagre substitute for chocolate. Listen to the chorus that sings in a rolling boil; picture your stomach sitting in a sidecar, propped against a leather jacket. Reduce heat to a simmer and

take off your hat. Take off a layer or two. Tie
a piece of twine in a bow around your pointer
finger and say *don't forget the oatmeal.* Smell the
sweat in a pot of chicken stock. Close the door
behind you and when you hear it shut, you'll
remember that you left your oatmeal in the
microwave years ago.

Liv spends Saturday mornings in her armchair with black coffee
and her book of crossword puzzles. She takes breaks from her
crosswords to watch people from her window. At 7:00 a.m., a
plump woman with a ten-year-old Chow Chow (that she insists
is purebred) walks down the street to the supermarket. Liv's apartment is across the street from a 50s themed restaurant called the
Atomic Diner. She watches as their servers arrive in poodle skirts
and high ponytails. Liv has never been inside, but every day she
sees people exit with milkshakes and root beer floats. At 8:30, their
delivery arrives. The delivery boy drops a tray of eggs he's pulled
off the bed of the truck. He picks up the tray and carries it into
the restaurant without even checking for breakage. At 10 a.m., a
man sits down on the curb in front of the diner and eats a cheese
bun; he caresses it the way Liv thinks he might caress a woman's
breast. Some Saturdays, a girl with short hair walks by with her
arms full of vinyl records and Liv feels her heartbeat quicken, for
a moment, forgetting that her stomach is empty. Liv likes to think
that she knows the people she watches, simply by virtue of having
witnessed their routines when they have not seen hers. She keeps
mental notes of what they wear, what they eat and to whom they
speak. The man with the cheese bun puts the remainder into
his mouth and shoves his weight off the curb. She doesn't know
where he goes afterwards, but she returns to her crossword. One
more clue, then she'll eat. 19 across—six letters—"to eat hungrily
or quickly (food or prey)," first letter D.

As Liv fills in the first letter, she hears a knock on the door. She assumes it's canvassers or a door-to-door salesperson trying to sell her a vacuum or a cheese grater. She ignores the knock, but within seconds, there's another. She scribbles the word DEVOUR into the last crossword squares, missing most of the lines, then wraps her shawl tighter around her shoulders. At the door, she puts her eye to the peephole and sees her mother in a floral shirt with a sweating, bearded man behind her. Liv takes a deep breath, counts down from five and opens the door.

> I've never understood anyone who can't eat alone in a restaurant; you see the most interesting people there. Once, the man at the table next to mine leaned over, tilted his half empty bowl of soup in my direction and said *the average soup spoon is the perfect size to cradle the human elbow. Unless your elbow is on the larger side, then you could always use a ladle.* He turned back to his soup and sipped from his spoon. I could hear it clink when it touched his teeth.

"Hello Olivia, how lovely to see you." She reaches a hand towards Liv's face as if she might pinch her cheek but decides against it and gives her a peck on the cheek instead. Her hand rests for a moment an inch from Liv's jawline.

"I'm surprised, Mother. You should have told me you were coming." Liv lifts her voice at the end of her sentence to make it sound less severe. She knows that doesn't work, so she tries to smile. Her mother ignores both of her failed efforts.

"I thought to myself, it's been far too long since I've come for a visit. With you living alone and everything, I thought about how lonely you must be. As soon as I thought about that—well, I just had to come."

Liv's mother leans on the handle of her suitcase and the man behind her shifts his weight between his feet.

"And this is…?" Liv gestures at the man lurking behind her mother. His body is too large for the space, but Liv can see him trying to make himself smaller by crossing his arms, which displays the wet crescents under his arms and draws more attention to the cramped doorway.

"Oh, this is my taxi driver. I didn't have quite enough to cover the fare. I *would have* had plenty, but the price of food on airplanes is just ridiculous. They had those awful little pretzels in foil bags. Foil bags! As if anyone could sleep with all that crinkling going on. The man beside me had *eight of them*. I can't imagine what he must have spent. Ordinarily, I never would have eaten them, but I was just famished."

The taxi driver clears his throat. "Just wait here a moment, sir."

Liv leaves the two of them in the doorway but hears the wheels of her mother's suitcase against her hardwood floor. Liv keeps her spare change in a pickle jar on top of the bedroom dresser. She starts to count out loonies and toonies, releasing the scent of vinegar with each coin. In university, Liv had an asthmatic roommate who coughed at the smell of vinegar, even at the mention of the word. He would twitch and get a pinch in his face if it were so much as used in a sentence and would eventually succumb to racking chest coughs. They decided to refer to it as the "v word" to save his lungs the strain. They'd had friends over for dinner one evening and Liv said to him, *can you pass the "v word."* One of their friends got a wrinkled look on her forehead and said *pass the vagina? I don't understand.* They'd laughed so hard that he ended up coughing anyway.

She realizes she doesn't know how much money she needs, so she puts the lid back on and tucks it under her arm like a football. When she comes out of her room, she finds her mother sitting in the armchair with the taxi driver leaning over her shoulder. They are looking at old photo albums. Liv doesn't have any photo albums; her mother must have brought one.

"How much do we owe you?"

Her mother is still pointing to pictures, explaining what disaster had happened with Liv's hair that morning, or how the photographer had turned out to be an old friend of hers. The two of them chuckle. Liv asks him about the fare again.

"It's twenty-five dollars, miss."

Her mother points to a picture while Liv counts out change, "Oh look at her there. My Olivia was such a round little child. And look at that little gap between her front teeth. She used to hate that."

The taxi driver laughs, too heavily, and small drops of spittle rest on his lip. He looks at Liv counting change and then back at the picture, comparing her to her old school photo. She remembers that photo, taken in the third grade before she'd gotten braces and appliances to close her tooth gap. She remembers placing a sliver of white bread between her teeth to give the illusion of a closed smile, but the photographer took one look at her and asked *are you saving that for later?* He told her to rinse her mouth out in the washroom so they could get some nice pictures.

"There, this ought to cover it. It was lovely to meet you, I'm sure you have somewhere to be."

The cab driver sniffs and clears his throat again, "This money... it smells like vinegar."

"Yes, it does. Have a nice day."

The taxi driver stands and straightens his pants where they've twisted around from sitting. "It was lovely to meet you, Elspeth and Olivia." He says their names slowly, the way one does when trying to remember whose company they're in. He shakes her mother's hand.

"Give my love to Bess and Catherine."

He nods, smiling, and lets himself out the door. Liv looks at her mother waiting for her to speak. When she doesn't, Liv twists the lid back onto the pickle jar and hoists it under her arm.

"Who are Bess and Catherine?"

"They're his kids. We got to talking in the cab and he told me all about them." Liv knows that her mother could talk about the taxi driver's children for hours, so she leaves the room to replace the pickle jar before her mother has a chance to begin. She sits on the corner of the bed and takes four calming breaths. She sniffs her fingers, which smell like vinegar too. She slips one of her fingertips into her mouth but finds that it tastes more like dirty money than vinegar. When Liv comes back into the living room, her mother is asleep in the armchair; Liv takes off her shawl and drapes it over the body of her snoring mother.

> I was taught about God by animated vegetables on TV, arranged by belief, not categorized by calorie count. The tomato told me the tired metaphor of rotten apples being the most symmetrical. After Sunday school, we went into the kitchen and were fed room temperature applesauce. I asked how I was supposed to tell the good apples from the bad ones if they were already mashed together. They told me not to take the lessons so seriously.

Liv takes the lock off the fridge before her mother can notice. As it uncoils, Liv wonders what she'll make her mother for lunch. She could leave to buy groceries, but what if her mother wakes up while she's gone? She'll come home and find her furniture rearranged and her floors polished. She wraps the lock back into a tight coil and tucks it into one of her lower cupboards, opens the fridge door and sees that her shelves are almost empty. She reaches a hand to the back and pulls out an old head of cauliflower. Its edges are brown and a small puddle of fluid remains where it sat. Wedged in between the back of the shelf and the back of the fridge is a pack of string cheese, but it's no fresher. Orange fluid seeps into the plastic around each piece. She knows she has a bag of potatoes stuffed in the bottom produce drawer, but she's hesitant to open the paper bag. They have eyes and are probably sprouting in the paper bag. She worries that moving the delicate balance of the bag will release the smell of rotting vegetables. She opens a cupboard and puts a box of strawberry Pop-Tarts on the table.

She leans back against the counter and looks up. She will not cry. Instead, she counts the watermarks on her ceiling.

"Olivia, please tell me that you haven't just been living on coffee and strawberry Pop-Tarts. You look so pale."

Her mother yawns, standing in the kitchen doorway with Liv's shawl wrapped around her shoulders.

"Of course, I haven't been, Mother. How did you sleep?" "It's a miracle I get any sleep at all these days."

Liv nods and feels the need to cry dissipating.

"Olivia dear, I have to ask. Where's the kitchen table?" Her mother stands where the table used to be with her eyebrows raised.

"It was taking up too much space. I sold it and bought a book-shelf." "You do realize that was my mother's table."

"I wanted to buy a bookshelf," Liv shrugs. "Where do you eat?"

"I eat in the armchair."

"You only have one chair, Olivia. Where am I supposed to sit?"

"You take the chair, I'll sit on the floor."

Her mother closes her eyes and pinches the bridge of her nose with her thumb and her pointer finger. When she stops pinching, a small red blotch spreads across her nose. "Well, no use crying over spilt milk, I guess. What's done is done. Now, what's for lunch?"

"Why don't we go out?"

"I think I'd rather stay in. I might fall asleep face down in my bowl. I'd rather do that at home than in a restaurant full of strangers if you don't mind. Anything you have is fine—anything *other* than strawberry Pop-Tarts."

Liv drags one of her kitchen chairs across the hardwood floor. The felt footpads lost their grip years ago, and the floor is scratched in a line from the table to the fridge. She'd tried filling them in with brown crayon, but she couldn't get the shade right. The closest she managed was a combination of *Raw Sienna* and *Beaver,* but the crayon wax left a film on the floor that caught and held breadcrumbs. The idea reminded Liv too much of flypaper, so she'd scraped the wax away and decided it would be better to live with the scratches. She parks the chair in line with the fridge and hoists herself up by the fridge door handle. She hadn't put locks on the cupboards because they were usually empty anyway.

> My mother and I sit by the garbage bins in the food court. Early Saturday mornings, it's usually us and a busload of senior citizens from the home down the block. I finish my breakfast sandwich and see that I've left a ring of red lipstick around the edge of my English muffin. I swallow a bite of my hash brown, then feel it turn to grease in my mouth. I force my tongue around the ball of potato and swallow. I feel it sink to the bottom of my stomach and settle against my sides. I have pockets of yellow fat under my skin, and they bulge out into the space around me. I distract myself by watching a woman in a polka dot romper. On the other side of the food court, she orders a hot dog for breakfast. I watch as she gets vertigo from standing too close to the hot dog rotator, catching its spin out of the corner of her eye. She recovers her balance, placing one hand against the counter and the other hand against her stomach. She smiles at the man handing her a hot dog and moves to a table to eat alone.

"Lunch will be just one moment, Mother." She sifts through the bundles of stained Tupperware containers and finally feels the shape of a can in her fingers: Alphagetti. She blows the dust from the top so she can see the expiry date. *Only one year expired*, she thinks. She climbs back down, keeping her thumb over the expiry date in case her mother decides to inspect the can; her mother worked for a food inspection agency for years. It made her the least interesting person at every party and meant that she never once went to a potluck.

"I suppose it will have to do. You know your apartment doesn't meet health and safety standards. You've got dishes in the sink, breadcrumbs on the counter, and how long has this coffee been sitting here? If this were a restaurant, I'd have to shut you down."

Her mother smiles and wiggles a finger at Liv, who yanks open the kitchen drawer and rattles the utensils inside to retrieve a can opener and a small saucepan. She scrapes at a few bits of food that are stuck to the sides of the pan, the metal feeling alien in her hands and her wrist aching at the weight. She puts it down on the stove and her fingers feel cold. Liv empties this morning's coffee into the sink and spoons out a few cups of ground coffee to make more.

"You know we have health and safety regulations for a reason, my dear."

Liv places the saucepan on the stove with a thud. She punctures the can lid with the opener and listens for the small release of air. As soon as the lid is punctured, the smell of Alphagetti reaches her nose and she winces—ketchup—her stomach begins to turn over. She reaches into the freshly unlocked fridge and takes out a bottle of sparkling water. She prefers sparkling water to still water because the bubbles give her the illusion that she's full, even though she's full of air. Her mind is filled with memories of summer barbeques, a picture of oranges on a vine. Liv holds her breath, bubbles in her mouth, and cranks the opener around the edge of the can, ripping off bits of the blue label.

> My mother told me that she was pregnant with twins when she had me. With Vanishing Twin Syndrome, there generally are no warning signs; one week two heartbeats, next week just one. The missing embryo usually dissolves back into

the mother's body. In rare cases, the second twin absorbs and consumes the embryo. Their skin cells can contain hair, teeth, and bones from the second fetus (eyes, torso, hands, feet, and other limbs, only in the rarest cases). In the twin that consumed the other, flattened pockets can remain undiscovered until much later in life. They rarely occur in other mammals but can be found in the occasional mountain lion.

Growing up, Liv and her parents lived down the street from a cookie factory. She could smell baking when she was waiting for the bus, but it didn't smell like the cookies she made at home. The air had a chemical smell, mixed with sugar, but that couldn't quite mask the fact that it wasn't natural. Some days on her way home from work, her mother would pick up castoff cookies. The factory managers put a pile of them at the service desk each day and customers could stop for the broken ones. Liv never told her mother, but she'd always wished that just once, she could have a whole cookie that hadn't been shattered or splintered into pieces. Her mother tried her best to piece them together using bits of icing, but it never worked. Liv's favourites were the fruit cream cookies, but those didn't break often. She thought that the small circle of jam provided the perfect amount of tension to keep the cookie in one piece. Her mother usually brought home plain tea biscuits. It wasn't that Liv disliked them, but she could make the fruit cream cookies last twice as long. She nibbled around them in a circle until she reached the jam in the centre, then peeled with her fingers and sucked until it dissolved under her tongue. Then, she could start the whole process over again. With the tea biscuits, one dip into a cup of tea and they'd break and sink to the bottom like ocean sediment.

The first night I spent with a man, he traced his fingers across the scar that stretches from my kneecap to my hipbone. Now it's pale and puckered—hasn't bled in years. When he asked me how, I told him that a dog chased me when I was ten. It cornered me and I had to jump over a fence to get away. I tucked pieces of strawberry into my cheeks as we spoke and prodded at the seeds with the tip of my tongue. I told him I slipped and cut myself on one of the wooden fence posts, but I didn't notice the cut until I got home and saw the blood pooling at my feet. I felt my stomach turn upside down and my head filled with air. I ran so fast that I couldn't feel my legs. His mouth made a small O shape as I spoke. In truth, I stood at the top point of the fence post to see how long I could stay there. I teetered up there with my arms in the air climbing an invisible trellis and stayed upright longer than I thought I could. Then the wind blew me over, and I fell.

"Olivia. Are you listening to me?"

It seems that her mother has been speaking, but Liv can't remember what she's said. Her mother has moved to the armchair and is completing one of Liv's crosswords in pen. Instead of muttering an apology for daydreaming, Liv takes the Alphagetti lid off, leaving a knife-sharp edge that perches like a hangnail. She's careful not to cut herself. A thin red line of tomato sauce dribbles down the label and settles on the counter. As she tilts the can over the saucepan, Liv feels its suction shift and the cylinder of soup drops with a sound like vomit hitting the floor. She remembers a news broadcast she'd heard about a family in Saskatchewan who found a cockroach in their can of Alphagetti. They'd filed a lawsuit against the company and after months of silence, the mother mailed the cockroach in an envelope to the CEO. Liv figures that she doesn't need to search for a cockroach, knowing her mother will give her bowl a thorough once over before she eats. Her mother sits in the armchair and clicks a pen in and out. She seems to be stuck on a clue.

A few of the letters stay in the can. If she were on her own, she'd dig them out with her fingers and see what she could spell with the leftovers. Since her mother is here, she takes a spoon from the drawer and scrapes them out one at a time. An R, an I, an A and an L dribble into the pot. Some of the soup stays in the cylindrical shape, the same way canned cranberries keep their rings in a bowl. Her mother taught her to always mash the cranberries until the rings disappeared, otherwise her guests would know that she'd used canned instead of making her own. To her mother, rings on cranberries were an unforgivable sin. She used to have a blackboard in the kitchen on which she'd written her "Ten Commandments of Eating." Number five was *Thou shalt never leave rings on canned goods when entertaining.*

Liv breathes through her mouth so she won't smell the Alphagetti and crushes the letters with the curved backside of a spoon.

"Mmm, smells great Olivia."

The skin around her mother's eyes wrinkles as she purses her lips. She clicks the pen and returns to the crossword.

My grandfather told me about a winter he spent working out in the bush before he met my grandmother. He said that the crows were tough and the squirrels were thin. He said at the worst of it, he could put his hand down his shirt and rest his fingers between the gaps in his rib cage. The feeling of skin surrounding his fingers brought some contentment, but he couldn't stay warm. He could place an almond in the crook of his collarbone and forget about it until he lay down in his cot and heard it roll to the floor. Out in the bush, you ate what you found, but some days there was nothing to find. *So*, he said, *I rummaged*. He tried to plant a grapevine behind his shed, but it only grew one grape that tasted like discount wine. He said he lost fifteen pounds, but he thought that he sweated most of the weight off with hard labour.

Liv picks up the saucepan and pours all of the Alphagetti into one bowl. She breathes through her mouth and tries to moisten her lips with her tongue. The letters clump together in the bowl. Liv remembers spelling her name with Alphagetti on the kitchen table when she was younger, digging letters out one at a time with her fingers and licking her fingertips when she'd laid the letters out on the table. She spelled her name, L-I-V, but she'd felt a presence behind her shoulder, a shadow over her bowl. Her mother asked her to dig out the other letters and spell her full name. Liv dug with her spoon to find the O, the I, and the A. When she spelled her name with all of its letters, her mother gave her a soft rub on the back. Liv felt the weight of her mother's wedding ring through her T-shirt.

"Why don't you go outside and play?"

Liv pushed her chair out from the table, scraping the floor, and wiped the orange corners of her mouth on her shirtsleeve. As she walked out the door, she turned and saw her mother swipe a crocheted dishcloth across the tabletop. When Liv came back home, the table was clean, her pot was washed and the dishwasher was running its familiar rattle.

Liv puts the bowl of Alphagetti on a tray she uses to store the TV remotes.

She takes it to her mother, who has given up on the crossword. "Bon appétit." Liv hands her a spoon.

"You're not eating?"

"I'm not hungry today."

> Once, I watched my mother reach her hand
> into the oven without a mitt. We were roasting
> pumpkin seeds to give to my class at school. I
> couldn't call out fast enough and I heard her
> skin sizzle where it touched the baking sheet. I
> was going to make a joke about needing adult
> supervision, but it didn't seem like the right
> time. My mother, who never cries, licked a tear
> that trailed down her cheek. She told me that
> her tears didn't taste as salty as they used to, then
> put her burnt hand under the faucet.

Liv turns the hood fan on. She still can't get the smell of ketchup
out of her nose. Her mother eats the Alphagetti one letter at a
time. Since her mother is in the armchair, Liv sits on a cushion
propped up against the leg of her coffee table.

Neither of them has seen any cockroaches so far. *There's still
time,* Liv thinks. Her mother never likes eating and talking, so Liv
picks up the book of crosswords from beside her mother's feet and
works on the one her mother hasn't finished. Her mother puts
a hand to her chest and clears her throat, pursing her lips into a
straight line and swallowing hard.

"Olivia, be a dear and fetch me a glass of water."

Liv puts her pencil in the crease of the crossword book and
hoists herself from the floor. As she runs the kitchen tap, she
wonders if she's poisoned her mother with the Alphagetti. She
figures it's unlikely, since the can was only expired, not dented.
She doesn't remember any dents, but she also doesn't remember
checking. She keeps the water running until it's cold enough that
it bites her fingertips. When she comes back to the living room
with the glass, the TV remote tray with the half-eaten bowl of
Alphagetti sits in the armchair and her mother is nowhere to be

seen. Liv takes her seat back on the floor and begins her crossword again. 15 across, six letters, "starchy plant tuber." Liv pencils the word POTATO into the squares. A few minutes later, her mother emerges from the bathroom and leans her forehead against the doorframe.

"I'm so sorry, Olivia. Something just didn't agree with me. I think I might lie down for a few minutes, if you don't mind."

Once her mother has left the room, Liv picks up the tray and drops the Alphagetti into the garbage can, bowl and all.

> My mother once spent a year almost entirely under water. She swathed herself in a fleece housecoat and wrapped the tie around her waist. In the mornings, she lifted her feet down the stairs and made herself a cup of coffee and then she waded her way back to the bathroom to fill the tub. She put her cup of coffee on the tiles, chipped grout, pulled herself out of the housecoat and pajamas limb by limb and lowered her body into the water. By noon, a wrinkled layer of buildup formed around the rim of her coffee cup like the scum on the edge of the tub. She traced the walls of the shower with stray hairs and curled them into spirals between the tiles. From above the water, her fingers looked thinner and her kneecaps poked out like mountaintops. I think she stayed under the surface to hear her stomach clatter against the ceramic tile. She told me once that she could feel the house shake when her stomach rumbled under the surface. I pictured her with sliced apples up her nostrils when she sank below the water.

While her mother sleeps, Liv puts the bike lock back on the fridge door, since the fridge looks naked without it. She takes a cookbook down from the second rung of her bookshelf; they'll have to go grocery shopping. Most of the cookbooks are her mother's. She dog-eared some of the pages when Liv first planned to move out. The ones she had folded down were her favourites—comfort dishes that Liv could make if she started to feel homesick. She folded down lemon meringues, rosemary potatoes, sage stuffing, apricot crostata, and eggnog cheesecake. On holidays, her mother spent all day in the kitchen and wouldn't let Liv help. From the living room, she would hear her mother speaking. Liv was never sure whether her mother spoke to herself or to the food she made. Liv sat down in the living room and peeled oranges. She liked to see how many pieces she could fit into her mouth at once, stacking bits of orange peel on the corduroy couch cushion next to her. She filled each crevasse in her mouth with orange pieces, until one of them finally burst and dribbled down her chin. When her mother called her for dinner, she spat the oranges into her hands.

For Christmas dinner last year, Liv cooked a chicken and mashed potatoes.

Since it was just for herself, she didn't make much. A friend told her to make friends with her food—to get comfortable with her food or try a food journal. She found herself explaining her recent breakup to her Christmas chicken, until she noticed condensation forming on its back as it defrosted. This is what she imagined her mother must have done with the turkey each Christmas. She tried the food journal instead, so she could have different conversations with her food. She started with aphrodisiacs; she thought they might be easier to write about. She'd written '*an ode to the truffle,*' but when she shared it with her friend, she realized she had misinterpreted the aim of a food journal. Her friend had calorie counts and nutrient percentages. Liv had poetry.

Liv starts to think about what to make for dinner but avoids every recipe with a folded corner. She takes the cookbook into the kitchen with her to take stock of her spice cupboard. The tang of ketchup hits her as soon as she walks through the doorway.

I finally found a seat in the bookstore where I could hide behind stacks of books. I pulled out my book and began to read when two women sat down with their arms full of cooking magazines. One of them pulled out *The Magic of Jell-O,* licked her fingertip and began to turn pages. *You know, this book is so right. There really are a million ways to make Jell-O interesting. Like tuna—now I know what you're thinking. Tuna? Never! But trust me. There's something about the two textures that just works.* I imagined that the Jell-O form on the cover of the magazine was sitting in front of me. In my imagination, I jabbed my finger through the surface and watched it crater.

Before Liv can stop herself, she remembers. Ants crawled through the folds and creases in her checkered blanket. Some of Liv's classmates had put dirt on their hamburgers then tried to eat them. Others unwrapped processed cheese slices, softened by the sun, to spread across their friends' faces. Liv sighed; the hotdogs were never warm, no matter how quickly they were placed in a bun. The power plant was across the street from her picnic blanket. In the books and fairy tales Liv read, picnics were held in meadows or pastures. Her parents sat with the other adults at a wooden table too small for their legs; they reminded Liv of Goldilocks in the 'too small' chair. Liv's mother wore a navy-blue sundress with a collared neck and a print of oranges strung on a vine. Liv knew that oranges grew on trees, not vines. Her mother said that maybe it wasn't a vine, it was thread and someone was trying to tie the oranges together into one long string. Liv thought about how difficult it must be to stitch pieces of food together like fabric.

Liv watched her parents from a swing set while she performed her experiment. She wanted to wrap all the way around the top bar of the swing, a full three hundred and sixty degrees. She got closer and closer each time. When she pumped her legs, her pants tugged at the seams and pulled at their stitches. When she swung, she felt weightless. Her hair blew behind her as she sliced the air towards the ground. It engulfed her face in a flurry of wind as she pumped her legs back up. In the moment the swing was at its highest, she felt like she would never come back down. She could pretend she was an acrobat hanging on by the tips of her toes, performing death-defying acts while everyone watched from below and cheered. *Lion Heart Liv's next trick will be her 360-degree stunt. Then next up, The Fattest Lady on Earth!* Liv kept a firm grip on the chains and pushed her legs out far enough in front of her to keep herself stable. She straightened her legs to begin pumping, slowly lifting higher and higher, inhaling so that she could really begin pushing. She bit down on her tongue when the air was shoved from her lungs and the swing came to a halt. The soles of her shoes rammed into the red gravel under the swing. The freckled boy had one hand wrapped around the chain, and one holding a piece of watermelon that dripped cloudy liquid down the side of his wrist.

> My mother and I carry the same weight. I carry mine in my face; she carries hers in her back. I threw out the scale and she brought it back to the ceramic tiles on the bathroom floor. She pulls out old clothes, disturbing the moths in the garage, and carries them up to the attic. She scatters them in a circle and stands in the centre. She opens a box of papers, shopping lists, recipe cards, and letters. She unfolds a letter that opens *Dearest one, I would eat your sadness if only I could.* She folds it in half and places it into the centre of her book, dog-eared at her favourite parts. She marks the middle point with a beef stroganoff recipe she pulled from a magazine.

The freckled boy had dared her. Liv needed to swallow one worm. Whole.

She couldn't mix it into her potato salad. She didn't want to eat potato salad anyway. The sun made it runny and moist. She kept the worm in a container until she was ready. For a little while, she sat with it and watched it turn and bend over itself. Liv felt a bead of sweat drop from her armpit and trail its way down her side. The worm occasionally lifted its upper half and stretched up, showing off its rings. She made sure to poke a hole in the top of the lid with the stick she had whittled into a point. Sitting on the edge of a wooden playground platform, she picked at a scab on her knee and decided that when she pried the scab off, she would eat the worm. When the scab finally loosened from her skin, she blew it off her fingertip and took a deep breath. A speck of blood pooled on her knee. She pried open the lid of the container, and the sun finally warmed it in her hands.

Around the corner from where she sat, a group of children spun in a circle, their white knuckled hands intertwined and smelling of playground gravel. The boy with the freckled hands sat in the middle. He'd stolen the whole bowl of watermelon and perched it on the ground between his crossed legs. He watched Liv without blinking and put chunk after chunk of watermelon into his mouth. He was sure she'd back out. The children chanted and he held a piece of watermelon in each of his freckled fists.

> *The queen of hearts she made some tarts all on a summer's day. The knave of hearts he stole the tarts and took them clean away.*

Their singing reached Liv's ears, but she was so focused she could barely hear. Liv inched her fingers toward the worm. Her thumb and index finger formed a pincer around the worm's centre. When she lifted it, the worm curved like an upside-down horseshoe and Liv could not tell which end was its face and which its backside. She did a quick check around her and saw her mother sitting with her legs crossed at the knees at the picnic table. It was so hot, she wondered if her mother would be able to uncross her legs when it came time to go home. From Liv's spot, the oranges on her mother's dress didn't look like fruit; they looked like polka dots. Liv tightened her grip around the worm, feeling it bend slightly under the pressure of her fingertips. She licked her lips, looked at the watermelon boy, then lifted the worm to her mouth and dropped it straight down her throat.

> *The queen of hearts called for the tarts and scolded the knave full bore. The knave of hearts brought back the tarts and vowed to steal no more.*

Liv closed her eyes and swallowed before she could feel the worm move in her mouth or her throat. She had a brief moment of satisfaction at proving the watermelon boy wrong, but when she opened her eyes, she saw orange spots everywhere. For a moment, she thought the sun had temporarily blinded her, but she felt a pair of hands grab at her face and pry her mouth open. She felt fingers push down her throat and then she felt the worm and all of the cold hotdog come back up. The children started another song and continued to spin, but the watermelon boy was frozen in place, with both pieces of watermelon partway to his mouth and moisture still dripping down his chin. Liv's mother handed her a handkerchief and told her to wipe her mouth.

"But Mom," Liv didn't recognize her own voice. It felt stuck in her throat like the round of a hotdog. She tried again, "Mom, I've done this before."

Her mother shook her head so hard that her hair came out from where it was tucked behind her ears.

"Never again. Never."

Her mother's lips formed a straight line as she handed her daughter another hotdog. Liv took the handkerchief and the hotdog but felt emptied. She placed the hotdog in the gravel beside her and hugged her bleeding knees into her chest.

When my grandmother died, we opened her closets and found seventy-two packs of double sized toilet paper rolls. The square bags nestled in next to one another without gaps in between. The neighbourhood kids started a rumor that she was a witch and didn't eat human food—she ate toilet paper. They said she didn't have teeth because she chewed cotton balls, which made them rot. Every day, she left a bowl of chocolate bars out on the front step so the kids could take some on their way home from school. When the sun began to set, she brought the bowl back inside to be emptied and refilled for the next day. I opened her bags of toilet paper, pulled squares off and separated the layers from one another, focusing on their softness between my fingertips. That's when the kids decided that I was a witch, too.

Liv finds herself rummaging through the freezer, knowing her mother might wake up if she turns on the light. She holds her cell phone up as a makeshift flashlight and her screen says 2:00 a.m. The light bulb in the freezer has never worked; somehow, before Liv moved in, it had melted into the base and couldn't be removed. She tried prying it out with a pair of pliers once, but it didn't budge an inch. She thought it might be a deterrent to rummaging in the night. Still, she knows that she is craftier than to be stopped by an obstacle as small as this. The light from her phone gives the contents of the freezer a blue aura. Liv holds the door open with her hip, which starts to ache because of the cold, but she is not finished. She finds four bags of frozen French fries and pulls the top off of each. She eats them one at a time, breaking them into small pieces with her front teeth. She winces when the frozen potato rests against her teeth for too long, but she doesn't stop. Half an hour later, she still holds the freezer door open, but unloads the rest of its contents into a black garbage bag. She feels the cold seep through the plastic. She takes her time tying the top of the garbage bag, finishing it with a perfectly symmetrical bow. Hoisting the bag up onto her shoulder, she opens the window and drops the bag. She listens as it hits the pavement with a thud.

The next morning, Liv's mother opens the freezer hoping to find the frozen waffles she'd seen, but instead finds only chunks of ice that cling to the door.

> A girl walks by our table. My mother turns to me and says *What an Unfortunate Body.* I sip my orange juice, feeling the acid slip down my throat. My stomach feels like it's waterlogged with potato, bacon, and lipstick. I wonder if I'm one of the unfortunate ones too.

Liv's class had gone to the museum to see the bugs. At the ticket booth, they each received a plastic wristband that gave them entrance to the exhibits, but as a class, they were only allowed to see "Bugs and Insects of Alberta: Pests or Friends?" The kids helped each other put on their wristbands, but some tried to do it on their own with their teeth. In the end, they each had a black band wrapped tight against their skin; tight enough that small beads of sweat formed on their wrists under the plastic. Their tour guide, Sandy, had a uniform one size too small and the kids thought she smelled like tomato soup. When she said that they could have a full hour at the end of the day to visit the gift shop, everyone but Liv cheered. She had already seen the gift shop when she came with her mother. Liv had walked by a display and tucked a bag of insect gummies into the pocket of her jacket. No one noticed the crinkling sound coming through her pockets, but Liv heard it pounding in her ears.

Liv got as close as she could to the display case, turned her lips into an "O" shape, and then breathed a small circle of condensation onto the glass. Before it disappeared, she drew an L with a loop in the middle with her finger. She smelled tomato soup emanating from behind her and an arm reached over. Sandy wiped the condensation off with the edge of her uniform.

"No touching, little girl."

Liv retreated to the red velvet bench and watched the other kids, who were fascinated with the exhibit. The one Liv really wanted to see was called "The Mysterious Bog People." Last time she was at the museum, her mother told her that the exhibit was too mature for a girl Liv's age but said that if it came back when she was older, they would go. Liv knew that meant never.

Liv waited until the other kids stood in line at the café for their lunch, pretending that their hotdogs and pizza slices were worms and stinkbugs. Liv ducked back below the red rope that separated the eating area from the museum and followed the signs to the exhibit. The closer she got to the bog people, the less she could smell the cafeteria food. When she reached the end of the signs, she found a door covered in what looked like ancient writing. Liv pushed and the door gave way with a creak. A film began as she walked into the dark room, a pale girl with blonde hair centered on the screen. She had no body that Liv could see; she was just a floating head on a black background. Liv's blood pounded in her ears and she only heard parts of what the girl said. *Nine years old… strangled…. could have been…* Liv felt her stomach lurch and she realized that she would be going without lunch. She did a mental calculation of the number of pieces of gum and the number of fruit snacks she had in her backpack. If she could keep the other kids away from her snacks, she would be able to eat quietly on the bus ride back to the school. Liv tucked the end of her braid into her mouth and sucked.

She had not been listening to the girl on the screen, but when she regained focus, the girl's face was no longer there. Her neck was contorted and hunched into her shoulder; her face was hollow and eyeless. A rope appeared around her neck.

No more words came through the speakers. The image faded to black as a row of light up arrows appeared under Liv's feet. She took a shaky step forward, steadying herself on the red rope as the arrows led her to a single clear case in the middle of the next room. It reminded Liv of the case where they had found Snow White, lying frozen with an apple in her hands. When Liv got closer, she saw that the girl's body was laid out, but not in the way Liv had expected. This girl was holding onto herself with her arms tucked in and her knees buckled, like they'd grown into one another. Her skin was wrinkled and crepe-like, without any hair. Liv felt pieces of her braid breaking off and realized she was still chewing on her hair. The girl's cheeks were sallow and looked hollower than human; Liv had not expected her to be so small. She began imposing the image of the pale girl in the video onto the body and began to wobble. She leaned against the end of the glass case and stared at her feet. When she looked at the girl's big toe, she saw that it was also hollow and crusted. It reminded her of the bubbles she saw on pizza dough her mother pulled out of the oven. Liv sat down with her back to the case and slumped over. She closed her eyes with her neck bent against her shoulder and her knees pulled into her chest.

> I use an egg timer as an alarm clock, waking to sour milk in my stomach. I yawn, but it sounds like I howl. My bones creak as I stand up to reheat yesterday's coffee—I tell it to stick to my ribs. When I go to the grocery store, my purse strap slides off my shoulder and my fingers get stuck in the baskets. I wish there were a cemetery nearby, because maybe I could go there for some peace and quiet.

Liv is kneading the dough between her fingers. Her mother has gone to the grocery store; she finished all of her crosswords and needs something to do. The bitter smell of yeast hangs in the air. She presses the dough into the kitchen counter and her wrist bones resist, flexing against the countertop. She dips her hands into the bag of flour and tries to scrape the counter with her nails, but the dough cakes as it dries. Flour floats to the floor as she moves, coating her arms and pant legs. She pulls her sweater over her head as she walks and hits her shin against the wooden leg of the armchair. The pain hits her all at once and she feels discomfort spread in the bottom of her stomach. Shuffling to the window, she throws it open even though it's twenty below. Pressing her flour-covered hands against the window frame, she breathes into the pain in her leg and knows she'll have a bruise in a few days. She smells the dough in the air and the powdery scent of uncooked flour. Across the street, smoke from the diner hangs in the air instead of dissipating like it would in the summer. The chill bites at her skin, but she smiles to herself as hairs on her arms lift with goosebumps. Liv sees a crow at the top of an evergreen tree, completely still and in the centre of the highest branch. Liv wonders how it keeps from falling, then she remembers that it'll fly if it teeters off the edge. Liv leaves the window open and turns back to her bread, biting at the dough under her nails and tasting only flour on her fingertips.

Growing up, Liv's mother had made bread once a week. Liv came home from school on Tuesdays to the smells of yeast and flour and felt comforted knowing that the bread would be baked by the time she finished her homework. Liv made sure she was home before the loaf made it into the oven. Each week, she'd lift the loaf and pinch a piece from the bottom. Molding the mass between her fingers, she warmed it until it was malleable enough to stretch without breaking. She pulled it as taut as she could, and then released it to see if it would stay loose. It reminded Liv of pulling a worm until it resisted and then watching its rings constrict as it pulled itself back inwards. Liv liked to tuck a piece of dough between her cheek and her teeth. She'd press in on her cheeks with her fingers and feel the dough settle between the spaces. After half an hour, she would spit the dough out onto the bathroom counter and admire the form of her teeth. Braces had twisted them until they were straight, but since having them removed, one tooth had migrated and crossed another on the left side. They were slightly yellowed with coffee stains but exceptionally straight, apart from that one tooth. She kept the remaining dough in a dresser drawer to suck on for the rest of the week.

When Liv was thirteen, she ate lunch in the school cafeteria. She would have preferred to eat in a classroom, but she'd watched kids bully one another for lesser crimes and middle school evils than that. She learned that bringing lunch in a Thermos was unacceptable after the fourth grade and the best way to fit in was to buy lunch from the school cafeteria. At noon each day, Liv lined up with her handful of coins, warmed by the sweat on her palms. She held them tight enough that Elizabeth II imprinted onto her palm. Liv knew that the cafeteria staff made the French fries days before and put them back in the deep fryer each morning. None of the other kids seemed to mind, so neither did she. Liv kept her change in her hand until she got to the front of the line and then reached for her fries in a paper cup. She wrapped her cup in a napkin, since grease dripped from between the seams and would cover her clothes if she weren't careful. Even so, by the time she found somewhere to sit, the grease had settled into the creases of her palm. Liv bought the lunch special each day from Lenora, a plump woman in a hairnet. She worked in the cafeteria in the mornings and wrote Harlequin romances in the afternoons and evenings. She smiled at Liv and sometimes winked as she tossed more fries into oil. Liv picked her French fries from the cup one at a time and left the bottom layer to sit in the grease. The cafeteria only had one window, a square cutout just below the ceiling, and no fresh air. Liv found it difficult to eat with so much chatter and the many aromas of different lunches, but she persevered.

Half an hour after lunch, Liv went to the bathroom on the second floor and knelt in front of the toilet bowl. She slipped the hair elastic from around her wrist, a red imprint spreading on her skin, and pulled her hair into a bun on top of her head. Taking a deep breath, she braced herself against the front of the toilet seat, then pushed her fingers into the back of her throat until she felt pressure from the pad of her index finger. She no longer gave in to curiosity by peering into the toilet bowl; she simply wiped her mouth on the cuff of her sweater and brushed the dust from her knees as she stood up. When she got home, she tucked a piece of dough in the space between her teeth and her cheek and filled her mouth.

Now, Liv kneads, knowing that she's over-worked the bread. She holds the dough in her hands, cupping it like she would a bird, heat radiating in her grip. She pinches off a piece and it leaves a tear, like a ripped piece of fabric. She touches the dough to the tip of her tongue and can tell that it doesn't taste right. It's sour and overheated from her hands. She presses it into the countertop, flattening it under the weight of her arm and it craters like Play-Doh.

Liv opens a drawer, rummaging under sandwich bags and twist ties, until she finds an old pack of cigarettes and a book of matches. She lights a cigarette and leans against the kitchen counter. The sourness in her mouth turns to mustiness, and she feels the rolls on her stomach tightening in on her like rope. Her hand shakes on its way to her mouth. Liv looks out the window at the tree where the bird sat and finds only an empty, perfectly still branch. Liv closes her eyes as Prufrock jumps up to the counter and licks the ball of dough. His black nose turns white with flecks of flour. She grinds the butt of her cigarette into the mass of dough, leaving a small, smoking hole, then hurls the whole ball into the garbage. She leaves Prufrock to lick the flour off the counter and walks to the bathroom to run a bath.

The newspaper headline reads *eighty-two-year-old man discovers lost wedding ring in carrot grown in his own garden*. He'd been planting carrot seeds, without gloves, and without taking his wedding ring off, and had lost it in the dirt. Years later, when carrots grew, they gave the ring back to him. In the picture, the carrot narrows in the middle, pinched, and strangled by the ring in its centre. He didn't pick up the phone to say that, all these years later, he found the ring. He put it in a cup on the mantelpiece. My mother threw her wedding ring out the front door when I was three. I wonder if her ring has sprouted into the roots of the tree, or if it's hanging off the edge of a branch, beckoning someone to take it.

Liv is covered in bubbles and feeling heavy in her arms as she pulls herself out of the tub. She takes a step and wraps her housecoat around her body, leaving puddles of water around her feet. She pulls her socks on, rolling them down to her ankles and as she stands up, recognizes the smell of cooking. She can taste meat in the air. Her stomach rumbles and she places a hand over her belly button to silence it. In her mind, she applies enough pressure to push straight through to her spine, but in reality, she can barely lift her arms without shaking. She forgot to turn on the fan and the room is full of steam. She tries to clear the mirror with her hand, but she can only see a vague outline of her face and features. She covers herself in lotion, taking as much time as she can. When she's done, the mirror has cleared enough for her to see that her skin is red and blotched across her nose and cheeks. She splashes cold water on her face and rubs her eyes. She takes small steps into the hallway, partly to avoid slipping on the puddles, but also because she doesn't know what she's about to walk into.

"Dinner's just about ready!"

Her mother's voice cuts through the steam in the air and Liv hears something drop into a cast-iron pan. The ensuing sizzle sounds like butter sputtering. Her stomach flutters. As she turns the corner, she sees her mother flipping two rib eye steaks into a frying pan. Liv tries not to think about burning flesh and bites her tongue, filling her mouth with saliva. She doesn't want to want this meal. When Liv looks away from the steaks, she sees that her mother is wearing an apron she bought in a pub in Nova Scotia years before. Liv hasn't had her radio on in the kitchen in months, but today, her mother has it on as high as the volume will go.

She leans against the counter with a glass of red wine in her hand and watches the steaks sputtering on the stove. A second full glass of wine sits on the counter.

When Liv went for her bath, her counters were covered in damp flour. Now, the counter is wiped clean, but Liv can barely see the surface. Her mother has stacked containers of rice three high, and the fruit bowl is overflowing with apples, oranges, and pomegranates. Liv can't imagine what the fridge must look like. She looks at it and notices that the bike lock has been removed. The only sign that it was ever there is a small scratch on the enamel, one that her mother has tried to cover with white out.

"I thought it might be nice for you and me to have a real dinner." The steaks hiss in the pan, spitting with herbs and melted butter.

"Since I'm feeling better, I figured I'd make us some dinner. You used to love rib eyes. Besides, your kitchen was so empty. I bought enough food for you to have three square meals a day."

Liv swallows, but her throat feels rough, like undercooked oatmeal. She tightens the housecoat around her waist and tucks her damp hair behind her ears.

"Why don't you go put on some clothes? Dinner will be ready in a few minutes."

Liv shakes her head and picks up the glass of wine from the counter, taking a sip that drains half the glass. She sits on the floor while her mother scoops dinner onto plates. Liv's old plates were white dinner sets, meant for camping, but her mother has bought her blue ceramic ones. She tries to picture what coloured plates will look like with different meals. She can't imagine an enticing plate of spaghetti on a blue plate. Blue is the colour of robin's eggs and dragonflies, not a dinner background. Her mother sits in the armchair and Liv sits on the floor, near the coffee table. Liv digs her fingernails into the grooves of the wood grain and runs them along the lines. Her mother has made a perfectly proportioned plate. The whole left side of the plate is covered in lettuce and cherry tomatoes. On the top right, she's put a half moon of wild rice with butter. On the bottom right, a steak cut into the exact size of a deck of cards. Liv's mother watches her daughter's calculations. She knows that Liv is calculating how many meals to skip to make up for this feast, or how many sit-ups wipe an ice cream scoop of rice off the scales. She also knows Liv is trying to find a way out—a napkin to slip half of her steak into, a way to call Prufrock to come and steal bits from her hand, wondering whether or not she can sneak a cigarette without her mother noticing. She still thinks her mother doesn't know she smokes.

Liv tucks a piece of damp hair into her mouth and grinds the strands between her teeth, coating her mouth in the taste of bubble bath. She flushes down the broken strands with wine. The dishwasher rattles, sounding like a spoon has loosened from the cutlery holder, pulsing with the water. She can see out the window from where she sits. The crow has returned to its top branch; it doesn't flutter its wings and it doesn't fall even as the branch sways in the wind. Liv tilts her head back to finish her glass of wine, noticing that her mother hasn't touched her own plate, but keeps both eyes keenly on her daughter. She holds her fork and knife in relaxed hands on either side of her body.

Liv takes a deep breath and pierces her fork into the steak, lifting it up off the plate in one piece. Her knuckles turn white and she says, "All right Mother, let's eat."

The alley behind my apartment is home to piles of fried chicken bones picked clean, broken fridge shelves with ketchup bottle scum, and single chopsticks with brown stains. My upstairs neighbours holler down the fire escape, and the smell of garlic wafts from their windows. I turn to my garden, choose an empty patch beside my fence, and fill it with soil from the hardware store. It's shaped like a trapezoid, about a foot wide on one side and a foot and a half on the other. I want to have a trellis leaning against the fence with peas and squash spiraling up, vines circling the splintered wood. I empty a bag of carrot seeds into my palm, place them one at a time into the earth, then cover them with soil. I take a dinner fork from my pocket and scrape the soil.

I want to watch something grow.

Wisteria

The sleepwalker will often have little or no memory of the event.

The coffee maker chugs to life, dripping watery specks into the cracked carafe. Franny keeps their coffee frozen in sealed containers because she believes that the cold keeps it fresh. Greg sits at the kitchen table, a clean mug in front of him with *World's Best Dad* screened across the ceramic, but the letters curve under his rough fingers so that only *est Dad* is visible. His other hand props a newspaper open to the obituaries. While his bran flakes soak in the milk, he runs a fingertip along the inked lines of the newspaper and mutters to himself. When the coffee maker beeps, Franny reaches across the table to fill his mug and tries to remember last night. A few grounds snuck through the filter, but Greg doesn't see them floating along the surface of his coffee. She takes a piece of brown bread from the freezer for her breakfast. Greg folds his paper and dips a spoon into his bowl.

"Do you ever hear me moving around in the night?" she asks him. With his cheeks full of cereal, he shakes his head. One speck of a flake migrates to his lip and trembles a little.

Franny scrapes the bottom of a peanut butter jar with a spoon as the toaster pops. She tries to spread what's left of the peanut butter on her toast, but most of it's gone or is slicked on her fingers.

She wipes her hands on her housecoat and takes a bite of toast, soggy in the middle from thawing in the toaster. Franny notices a hole in the shoulder of Greg's sleep shirt, a patch of greying skin showing through. Before, Franny would have stitched it closed. He sips his coffee and delicately licks his unshaven upper lip, nearly catching the stray bran flake.

"Do the kids ever say anything to you about my sleepwalking?"

He stares at the flakes floating in the bowl.

"Greg, do you *know* that I sleepwalk?"

He puts down his spoon.

"Franny," he pauses to swallow, "you nearly climbed out the hotel window on our honeymoon. I'm not likely to forget pulling you back in through the curtains, am I?"

He laughs. She chews her toast, tasting only the thinnest coating of peanut butter.

Before the kids stumble into the kitchen, Greg says, "you should probably see someone about that. It might be hereditary."

The kids enter, still sleepy in their pajamas. They sit around the table with a wilting branch of wisteria in the centre.

Psychological interventions have included psychoanalysis, hypnosis, scheduled or anticipatory waking, relaxation training, management of aggressive feelings, sleep hygiene, or electric shock therapy.

Greg and Franny met in the autumn of '97 when he worked as a leaf blower for the University of Toronto. She was on her way to the library when she saw him cutting across the field with the leaf blower strapped to his back. A hose and cables were wrapped around his midsection and he wore an old pair of lab goggles for protection. Franny watched him for a few minutes, noting the flecks and leaves stuck in his hair, the patches of sweat spreading across his back. She had just begun a teacher-training program after finishing her degree in botany. When she'd finished her placements and fall turned to winter, there were barely any leaves left to blow. She spoke to him. He moved in with her three months later.

She finished her program but hadn't taught in a classroom before discovering that she was pregnant. She lined the pregnancy tests up on the bathroom counter and couldn't help but think, *I am germinating; I have a seed in me.* She slept in the baby's room for months after the birth, sitting upright in an armchair by her daughter's crib. In the night, she had to keep her hand on the baby's stomach, or else she would cry. Franny closed her eyes and pretended to sleep so that the baby might sleep too.

Franny and Greg have two daughters, Helen and Kate, who are seven and nine. Kate wants to be an astronaut and Helen wants to be a writer. They eat their sugary cereal each morning and Franny picks at her cuticles, knowing that she won't stop picking until she bleeds. Greg reads the obituaries.

Night terrors are a disorder related to
sleepwalking. They tend to run in families.

Franny has heard all the stories about sleepwalkers. A woman in France once painted a masterpiece in her sleep. A man in Edmonton drove ten miles to pick up milk and only woke up when the cashier told him he had the incorrect change. Each night, she falls asleep and her things are in the right place, but when she wakes up, everything is different. Franny has woken up with her botany books off her shelf and dog-eared at different places, or her housecoat circling through the washing machine in the basement when she knows she left it on the hook in the upstairs bathroom. Her door stays shut with a piece of string, tied between the doorknob and her bed. In the morning, it's been cut cleanly in half.

Tonight, Franny finds herself sitting straight up at the end of her bed. She has a vague memory of her lips forming words, but to whom? She doesn't know. Franny pictures what someone would see if they came into her room and found her sitting there, feet planted firmly on the hardwood and her veined kneecaps showing beneath the hem of her nightgown. They might assume she was praying, forming the bulky shapes of words with her lips. Rooted to her quilted bedcover, she tries to mentally place herself back in her bedroom, settling into the softness of the bed and the chill in the air through her open window. The window was shut when she went to sleep. She reminds herself that she is not wearing a ball gown in an antique theatre. She is not seated at a restaurant to celebrate her birthday. Her body is not upright in a chair, hands clicking away at a typewriter. She unsticks her legs from the quilt and crawls back under the covers, cooled in her absence. A toenail catches the threads of her sheets when she shifts underneath; she'll try to remember to trim it tomorrow.

Sleepwalkers should talk to their doctors or a sleep specialist about ways to prevent injury during an episode and about possible underlying illnesses.

For the first few years, Greg had often bought flowers to put in the vase on the kitchen table. He used to bring daisies, yellow roses, and dahlias wrapped in brown paper. Now, he cuts branches from the wisteria plant that climbs the outer walls of their house. They wilt within a day or two and release a heady smell that reminds Franny of her grandmother's house. Once they've wilted, she throws them into the compost where they stay until the bins are emptied on Sunday. Friday nights are family dinners and they sit around the wilting wisteria branch to tell the same stories and laugh at the same jokes. They sit around the table, laughing and throwing their heads back while bellowing. It reminds Franny of when she was a girl, walking by clusters of men outside bars and barbershops. They would laugh collectively and Franny would feel herself shrink, walking as quickly as she could to get away.

She reads the ingredients on the frozen pizza box, trying to memorize and recite them back to herself. *Wheat flour, water, rye flour, bacterial cultures, salt.* They can continue the conversation without her.

"Do you have to read everything, Franny? Come and join us."

They laugh and she watches the pizza in the oven, cheese bubbling and breaking in the heat.

*Remove any sharp or breakable objects from the
area near the bed, install gates on stairways, and
lock the doors and windows in your home.*

She is staring at the hole in his sleep shirt, large enough for a finger to fit through, but not large enough for him to notice or replace it.

"I don't want flowers anymore, Greg."

He sits up on the couch and repeats her words, but they fit differently coming from his lips. He phrases them like a question he doesn't understand. Franny has no memory of leaving her room, or of gripping the railing as she came down the stairs, or of putting the kettle on to make the cup of tea she holds in her hands. The alarm clock on the coffee table says 2:09 a.m. Franny notices the curvature of his body molded into the couch cushions.

"I don't know what that means, Franny," he says, rubbing the heels of his hands against his eyes.

She sits on the edge of the couch and hands him the cup of tea. Greg sips from the mug, then yawns. He looks like a boy under the blanket that's big enough for a king-sized bed. The fabric tucks into the folds and cracks of the small leather couch. After a few minutes, he puts the empty mug on the floor and lies back down. He watches as Franny places a hand on his stomach. He feels her palm, formless and warm from the cup of tea she brought. He keeps his eyes open for a few minutes, and then settles into sleep and a predictable pattern of breathing.

Franny was five years old the first time it happened. She left her bed, trailing a blanket behind her and woke up on her front lawn staring up at the chestnut tree. Her mother had heard the front door open and saw Franny through the cracks in her blinds. She coaxed her daughter back inside and made her a cup of tea, wrapping her in a blanket from the hall closet that smelled like cedar and mothballs. The blanket that Franny had taken outside was covered in burs that pricked her fingers when she'd tried to pull them off. Miniscule beads of blood formed and spread on her fingertips before her mother took it away. Her mother had put stronger locks on the windows and doors, but in the end, it wasn't important, since that was the last time Franny sleepwalked until her honeymoon.

Wharf

"Anybody want to go for a swim?" Holly already had her running shoes off and a pair of rubber flip flops in her hands. "It's too fucking hot in here and that raccoon makes me want to barf."

Caleb found the raccoon behind the generator our first day at the cabin. He took a branch from trees by the water, tied it to the raccoon corpse, and propped it up against our cooler so it looked as though the raccoon might reach in and grab a bottle of beer. The four of us were splitting the cost of the cabin, but I only really knew Caleb. We were close in high school and had kept in touch, but this was my first time spending more than a couple of hours at a time with him since our first year of university. We would meet at the campus bar for a pint and some fries. When he invited me to join him and some friends at a cabin for a week, I thought it might be a good way to celebrate finishing my degree. Let off some steam. Make some friends. Put off the inevitability of trying to find a job. Holly looked at the raccoon and faked a gag as she pulled off her tee shirt to reveal a bikini top. I didn't have a problem with dead things as a rule, but I also knew that decomposition would begin in earnest in the coming days. I could try to convince Caleb at least to move the raccoon outside.

"Just give me a second to change," I said, taking my bathing suit out of the backpack I'd dropped at my feet. Daniel laughed in a way that didn't reach his eyes.

"Dude, we don't have any secrets here. Just strip down so we can get to the lake faster."

He unzipped his shorts, pulled off his boxers, and slid a pair of swim trunks over his slim hips, but not before I could see his fully naked body. Caleb took off his shirt—he turned away from me when he took off his pants so that I only saw his backside. I wished I'd had Holly's foresight to wear a bathing suit beneath my clothes.

"Seriously," Caleb said as he turned around, "it's fine, no one cares what you look like naked."

I began to unzip my denim shorts and tried to remember what kind of underwear I'd put on that morning. I gripped my bathing suit and shimmied it up my legs as quick as I could while looking at the floor. When I was fully covered again, I looked up and locked eyes with Daniel.

"That wasn't so bad, was it?" He winked at me on his way out the door and turned back. "Nice scar, by the way." I had a thin, puckered scar on my upper thigh from a fence jump gone wrong in junior high. Holly was already heading down the dirt path that would take us to the lake. She didn't look back to make sure we were coming. Daniel followed behind her.

"We really should move the raccoon outside," I said to Caleb. He rolled his eyes at me as he grabbed some beers from the cooler, picked up the raccoon by the stick and carried it over his shoulder and out the door.

"Race you to the wharf," he said as he deposited the raccoon beside the welcome mat and handed me a beer.

"You're on," I said but Caleb was already running ahead of me, kicking up dirt on the path. I knew my beer would be shaken beyond all hell by the time I got there, but I ran anyway. When I got to the lake, I was winded and had dirt in my eyes. They felt like the sandpaper my dad used to strip varnish from old furniture. The others were all lined up on the edge of the dock, waiting for me to jump in with them. I dropped my things, ran towards them, and pictured this moment as though it were the end of a movie where we hold hands, count down from three, and jump into the lake as the sun sets. This was not that moment. Caleb belly flopped, I jumped straight down, and only Holly and Daniel held hands. When I resurfaced, the cold froze my lungs for a moment before I remembered how to breathe. Holly bobbed up and wiped wet hair from her face with her hand. Daniel and Caleb were still under. I reached out to grab at the rotting wood of the dock when I felt something solid and heavy swish against my legs in the water.

"That's not funny," I said to no one in particular since whoever was under the water wouldn't be able to hear what I said. I looked over at Holly who was floating on her back and not paying any attention to me.

Caleb's head popped up about twenty metres away. He smiled at me and I couldn't smile back because I was waiting for another sensation beneath the water. I grabbed at the dock again and began to hoist myself up when I heard and felt a splash behind me and hands wrapped around my hips to pull me back under. I sank beneath the surface, lake water in my nostrils and an immediate burning. I managed to wrench myself free from the arms that held me under and kicked my legs until I got to the surface. Daniel bobbed up about a meter away from me.

"Dude, you kicked me in the stomach," he said, but it was obvious by his grin that he wasn't hurt.

"You pulled me under." As soon as the words were out of my mouth, even I could hear how watery they sounded. Like I was on the verge of tears. Or a meltdown. Or a tantrum.

"Did you get a little scared?" This time I grabbed at the wooden dock and hauled myself out before anyone could pull me under. I picked up my beer from where I had left it and took a long swig to wash away the taste of lake water and dead fish that burned my nostrils and throat. I heard the others getting out of the water shortly after me and swallowed down the shaken beer.

I watched Holly and Daniel leave the lake hand in hand and follow a smaller path than the one we'd taken to get there.

"Try not to let Daniel get to you too much. He's just a joker. He's a pretty good guy once you get to know him." Caleb sat down next to me and dried his hair with my towel. I nodded and tried to blink the sunblock and water out of my eyes.

"What have you been up to these days, anyway? It feels like a long time since we've had a real talk," Caleb said. Our conversations at the campus bar were mostly surface level: how our parents were doing, memories from high school, how many midterms we had to study for.

"Not much," I said. "I finished school. My dad tried to get me a job at his company, for the summer at least, but they put a freeze on any new hires."

"Bummer."

"Yeah. I'll start looking for a job next week."

I didn't tell Caleb that I'd been offered a job at my dad's company, but I couldn't accept it. It wouldn't be fair to them. I might even be a liability.

"I'm sure you'll have no problem getting hired."

"We'll see," I said.

Mid-way through my last semester, I walked out of the biology building which felt almost tropical and into the February air. My lungs constricted, my muscles froze, and I couldn't breathe as soon as I stepped into the minus thirty-five courtyard. My hands went to my throat and someone nearby thought I was choking. I managed to run back inside and into the warmth of the building where my lungs remembered what to do. After that, I didn't need a cold rush to freeze. It just happened.

"Still no word from your mom?" he asked.

"Nothing yet."

Caleb knew the sparsest details about my family situation. My dad came home from work one day and my mother had gone. She'd packed up her things and left a note telling him that there was two weeks' worth of meatloaf in the basement deep freeze. What Caleb didn't know was that there was another note with the name and phone number of every hook up and one night stand my dad had ever had while he was married to my mom. He thought she didn't know. He thought I didn't know.

"What about you?" I asked.

"I've decided I'm not going back to school," Caleb said. I swallowed a sip of my beer which was getting warmer by the minute and wasn't completely clearing the taste of lake water from my tongue.

"How did your old man take the news?"

"I haven't told him yet. I'm planning to tell him next week. I just... I can't go back there for another year."

"Hold that thought," I said, "I have to pee."

I didn't really have to pee, but school had been a tricky subject for Caleb and me since our first days in a high school biology lab making gene charts with markers. Knowledge came to me naturally—I could memorize information, I did well on standardized tests, my parents never had to come to parent-teacher interviews. Caleb, however, had always struggled. I learned not to ask.

I followed the same small path that Holly and Daniel had taken. I figured I would wait a few minutes before going back and then I could change the subject with Caleb. Transition into safer territory. I stopped a reasonable distance away from the lake and leaned against a tree, kicking at the roots with my flip flop. I looked up when I heard voices. Holly and Daniel were about twenty feet away, still holding hands and it didn't look like they saw me. The trunk of the tree was wide enough that I could stand behind it and be fully blocked from view.

I couldn't move. I wanted to, I really think I did, but my legs were tangled with the roots beneath me. I watched as Daniel stopped walking and pulled Holly towards him. When she was facing him, he put his hands on her shoulders and pushed her down onto her knees. He took one hand from her shoulder to undo the ties of his swim trunks and to shift them down a few inches until I could see the dimples in his lower back. Holly took off her sweater and rolled it beneath her knees so they wouldn't get scuffed in the dirt and branches of the forest floor. She took a hair tie from her wrist and whisked her wet hair up on top of her head. Even from twenty feet away, I could hear Daniel moaning in time with the movements of Holly's mouth. He wrapped his hands around the back of her neck, pushing himself in, and after a few more minutes, I watched him plant his feet and shudder.

Holly wiped her mouth with the back of her hand. Daniel pulled his swim trunks up, leaned down and kissed Holly on the forehead. It was like the disconnection of their bodies finally allowed mine to move. I shifted against the tree and a branch snapped beneath my foot.

"Did you hear that?" Holly asked.

"Hear what?" Daniel still sounded out of breath.

"I think there's someone nearby."

"Probably just a raccoon or a deer. Come on, let's get back in the water."

They went in the opposite direction from where I stood. I waited a few more minutes, just in case they came back, and was about to retrace my steps to the lake when I noticed a flash of pink on the forest floor. Holly had left her sweater. It still bore the imprint of her knees. I picked it up, shook out the brambles and pine needles, and tucked it under my arm. When I got back to the lake, I heard raised voices, but I couldn't distinguish words until I got closer.

"Dude, that's not a wharf."

"It *is*." Caleb's voice had the same watery quality as mine.

"Wharves have places for boats to moor. This is just a dock," Daniel said as he reknotted the ties of his swim trunks.

"I know what a wharf is. I'm telling you; this is a *wharf.*"

"It isn't man. I don't know how else to tell you."

"Do you think I'm stupid? Is that it?" Caleb's face looked like he had been sunburnt.

"I'm just saying if you can't tell the difference between a dock and a wharf…"

I remembered the look on Caleb's face—it was the face I'd seen after we finished writing our diploma exams. Mine would lead into an honours program, but Caleb spent years upgrading until he had the minimum grades necessary for university admissions. I was proud of him, but I don't think I ever told him that. He'd had to work a hell of a lot harder than me to accomplish anything. But watching Caleb's face redden, I knew what would come next. Caleb had never hit me, but I'd seen him hit others. I ran to the edge of the dock and put my body between theirs.

"Daniel, let him cool off." Holly watched from a safe distance and I knew I couldn't rely on her for any kind of backup.

"What are you—his girlfriend?"

I held my ground and spread my legs a little wider to take up more space.

Daniel looked me up and down and I realized what he saw but I realized it too late—Holly's pink sweater was still crumpled in my fist.

"You little creep, you were watching us, weren't you?" I looked down at my flip flops. "Well? Weren't you?"

"I—"

"Fuck you."

I felt his hands on my chest, the ones I had just seen around the back of Holly's neck, and I was falling backwards, into the water, and then sinking. I couldn't move. I wanted to, I really think I did, but I couldn't compel my legs to kick or my arms to make any kind of motion. The only thing I could do was look up—to see the body of a small, dead fish floating at the surface and lines of light stretching downward. I reached the bottom of the lake and could sink no further. I couldn't tell if the surface of the water was ten inches or ten meters away, but it didn't matter. I felt my feet sink into the algae, and the rocks, and the dirt, and I thought: perhaps I would stay.

Body Fluid Spill Kit

*You will pour out and wonder
if your body has been swapped
for a wooden board. But you move.
You move and move and move. You
scatter and you won't know where you
land until you hit the ground*

🖐️

When Evelyn turned her head to shoulder check, she was startled by the presence of a body in the back seat. She'd wanted to merge onto the 53rd avenue exit on Crowchild Trail and had already begun her move when the sight of the body sent her swerving back into her original lane without shoulder checking. An SUV behind her honked before speeding past—the man in the driver's seat (with a face like an uncooked T-bone steak) glued his eyes to Evelyn's as he slowly lifted his middle finger. The finger went higher and higher and Evelyn hoped he might miscalculate space, time, and distance, to momentarily lose his sense of spatial awareness until the finger went right up his nose. She wanted to see him knuckle deep. No such thing happened.

That wasn't very good, was it? the body in the back seat asked. Evelyn looked in the rear-view mirror and could see that it truly was a body—when it spoke, words scraped from its throat like an electric can opener. She'd bought one for her mother when the arthritis got worse and she couldn't grip a manual opener or twist the lid of a jar. The electric opener arrived a week before Evelyn's mother died. When Evelyn went to the house for the first time after the death, there was a can of Campbell's cream of celery soup hanging from the ridge of the opener. There was a gash from a knife in the top of the can. Evelyn flipped the switch and it turned a quarter inch in one direction and then a quarter inch in the other. It created a hole in the can—a hollow place—but not enough to remove the lid. She wondered how long her mother had persevered with the electric opener before pulling a knife from the drawer and hacking away at it only to put it back on the malfunctioning machine. Evelyn wiped bits of celery from the rim and mailed the opener back to the manufacturer. She did not request a replacement.

Evelyn stayed on Crowchild and took the opportunity to examine the body further by glancing in the rear-view mirror.

The body's eyes were cloudy and slightly deflated, but still in the skull. This deflation reminded her of Mia's ninth birthday party—her daughter. Evelyn had invited all of the neighbourhood children—even Trevor from down the street who chewed his own toenails. Not one of them came. Over the course of the afternoon (and the following afternoon and the following afternoon), the birthday balloons deflated until they were covered in tiny wrinkles that reminded Evelyn of elderly pugs, but Mia didn't seem to mind.

Evelyn briefly wondered who could have taken the care to buckle a body into the backseat like a child when she remembered she was still on Crowchild Trail, barreling past the next viable exit and well on her way to Tuscany.

Should we stop for coffee? You look like you could use some, the body said.

"We don't have time for coffee. Not today." She couldn't help but notice the stitches along the body's sternum in a long Y shape and she wondered if the stitches were watertight. "Can you even drink coffee? Won't it just pour right back out of you?"

I can drink coffee.

"Fair enough."

She needed to get off Crowchild Trail and turn around, which would take her past at least four coffee shops anyway. If she wanted to make it through the day in one piece, she would need caffeine and simple carbs.

*One day you will find yourself buckled
into the back of an SUV with no
memory of how you got there. You
will not feel the same. Your body
will feel like a stranger's. You will
not know what you had for breakfast
(or if you even ate breakfast) or
what you did the night before (or
if you did anything the night before) or
how many hours you slept (or
if you even slept at all). You will
be vacant. You will try to speak
but the sounds from your mouth won't
be the same. You will feel the movement
of a car, the pressure of a seat belt against
your chest, the tugging of stitches you don't
remember getting. You will close your
eyes. You will do your best.
But it won't be enough.*

Evelyn had received a call from the principal's office at her daughter's school. According to the woman who handled school admin, (she reminded Evelyn of Danny DeVito), Mia had been caught snipping bits of other kids' hair with scissors when they weren't looking. Nearly the entire grade four class had a chunk of hair missing from the back right side in some perverse, reversed, and unintended mullet. In October, the janitor found a box of teeth in Mia's desk—no one knew where they had come from, but the janitor said the patterns and grooves on the teeth indicated that they could have been human (no one asked why the janitor knew so much about teeth). In November, Mia had stolen the body fluid spill kit from the school bus on a field trip and used the absorbent powder to create potions. When Trevor (the toenail biter) puked as the bus took a particularly hard turn, there was no kit strapped to the wall—the vomit roiled around beneath seats catching backpacks and shoes indiscriminately. The teachers pulled pocket packs of tissues from their backpacks and did their best, but it wasn't enough.

Evelyn wasn't surprised by the body in the backseat—to be honest, she'd wondered when something like the body might appear. Strange things had been happening for the past few months. A dead grackle on the windowsill that she didn't want to handle stood up, shook itself off, and flew away despite the gaping wound in its chest. There had been shadows in the corners of picture frames and bits of light reflecting on walls—Evelyn could never find the source even when she closed all the blinds. Mia had been talking in her sleep about summoning demons. Evelyn figured this was all culminating in some great emotional revelation or a complete breakdown.

All of this aside, the body was right—she could use some coffee.

The body in the backseat didn't move much when it spoke, only the lips curled slightly as they formed words and Evelyn could see the tip of its tongue flicking front teeth when it said a word like *look* as it lifted a hand and pointed at a police car on the side of the road ahead. Evelyn checked her speedometer and dropped her speed by ten. The body pressed its hand to the window and Evelyn imagined the handprint it would leave behind with fingerprints and oils and skin.

They pulled into the Starbucks parking lot and Evelyn nearly closed the door behind her before remembering the body.

"Did you want anything?"

One of those little vanilla scones if they have them.

"Nothing to drink?"

No thank you, just the scone.

"I thought you said you could drink coffee."

I can, but that doesn't mean I want to.

Evelyn closed the door and locked the car behind her.

It was only as Evelyn ordered a petite vanilla bean scone and an Americano that she realized the appearance of the body would be cause for concern to almost anyone else.

"Make that two vanilla scones, please. And another Americano." If Evelyn was going to be late, she may as well bring coffee for the principal too (none for the Danny DeVito lookalike). It would probably be interpreted as ass-kissing, but Evelyn didn't care.

The barista handed over a paper bag and Evelyn moved to the side to wait for her coffees. She wondered if anyone in the parking lot would walk by her car and see the body. Would they call the police? Or would someone think the body was just sleeping after a night out and looked a little worse for wear? She surprised herself by hoping that the body would still be there when she returned.

When Evelyn walked back to the car with a coffee in each hand and the bag of scones tucked under her armpit, she found the body exactly where she'd left it, buckled into the seat and leaning against the door.

"One vanilla scone for you." The body lurched forward to take the scone—Evelyn had assumed that the atrophy of muscles would inhibit movement beyond the brief hand lift she had seen before.

Like an unnaturally large marionette, the body took the scone from the bag and ate it in small nibbles. As Evelyn watched, it looked out the window and seemed to fixate upon an empty shopping cart someone had left in the middle of the lot. The wind blew and the cart travelled a few inches toward a puddle of slush. The cart would likely remain there until the end of winter.

"Well," said Evelyn, "let's get this over with." She pulled out of the parking lot and once again merged onto Crowchild Trail. "It probably isn't even Mia that's cutting hair." But she knew it was Mia. Her daughter had been tying bits of hair together with twine in the backyard and hanging them from the lower branches of their willow tree. Evelyn hadn't asked where the hair had come from, it was just there. Now, some strange primordial defense mechanism made her stand by her daughter at least once, if only to the body.

Do you know what you'll tell them? the body asked.

"I'll tell them the truth. That Mia has been having a hard time adjusting since her grandmother died."

But that isn't really true, is it?

"What do you mean?"

I mean it started before your mother died.

"Yes," Evelyn paused, "but it's gotten worse since then."

I suppose that's true, said the body. It lifted its right hand to its lips and licked remnants of vanilla icing from the fingertips. *Are you going to punish Mia?*

"I don't know yet."

The body didn't say anything. The only sound in the car was the slight wheeze the body made between breaths (but were they breaths? Evelyn wasn't sure. She tried to watch the body to see if it was breathing without looking like she was checking for breath. She didn't know if that would be offensive to the body, so she looked as subtly as she could).

You will not remember what happened to you.
You will think you were old but you aren't sure
because the markers of age have mostly disappeared.
Your muscles will not feel taut. They will feel like
over-used elastic bands. You will not be sure why
the woman in the car speaks to you as though
she does not know you. Because you know
her. You just can't remember how.

Evelyn signaled and merged onto the 53rd avenue exit. This time the traffic lights from further up the road cooperated—there were no other drivers nearby. Evelyn shoulder checked anyway and noticed that the body had closed its eyes. The lids were the colour of eggplant skin.

"You okay back there?"

Yes, why wouldn't I be?

Evelyn heard the persistent click of the turn signal she had forgotten to shut off.

"You were just awfully quiet."

You always were uncomfortable with silence.

"No, I'm not."

You are. You like to talk. You fill the void with words.

Evelyn turned her eyes back to the road. She didn't need to defend herself to the skin sac in the back of her car. But something nagged at her and it wasn't just *what* the body said, but *how* the words were conveyed. There was something familiar and Evelyn couldn't put her finger on it.

"Why do you think you know anything about me? Because we stopped for coffee?" Silence in the back seat. "Because, for some reason, you're in *my* car and I'm only late because of having to deal with you all morning on top of everything else?"

The body responded with a wheeze like part of the airway was blocked.

"I hope you're gone by the time I get back."

Evelyn pulled into the school lot and parked next to a Mini Cooper with a snow-covered windshield and an anatomically incorrect penis drawn into the slush.

"Let's get this over with."

She didn't lock the doors behind her.

In the first week of September (what turned out to be her mother's last trip to the zoo), Evelyn's mother had ruffled Mia's hair and nearly knocked the faux-fur bear ears off her head. Mia had insisted on wearing them. Evelyn didn't know what she expected from the bears—some kind of recognition? Kinship? A connection? She knew Mia would be disappointed when they got to the enclosure and found the bears asleep, missing, or tempted by food in an inside room. Mia would cry. Her grandmother would pat Mia's eyes with a Kleenex.

A zookeeper spotted Mia with her bear ears and came up to Evelyn. "Your daughter is *charming* in those ears."

Evelyn knew how charming her daughter could be. Once, Mia told a security guard at the mall that she had been kidnapped and that Evelyn wasn't her real mother. When they were back in the car and Evelyn had exhausted herself with disciplining as best she could, Mia smiled and asked if they could stop for ice cream on the way home.

"Hold this." Evelyn's mother held out her handbag, but Evelyn watched Mia as she tried to climb a fence to gain access to the enclosure. For a moment, Evelyn wanted her to make it over the top.

"Evelyn, did you hear me?"

"Yes, mom. I did."

"Well, why didn't you say you heard me?"

Evelyn took the handbag and lifted the lid off her coffee cup. Maybe one or two remaining drops would take pity on her. There were none. Her mother rubbed lotion into her elbow skin and hands, then reached toward Evelyn for her bag.

"How has Mia been doing in school?"

"Fine. Why do you ask?" Evelyn knew she had asked too quickly.

"I will never understand how I raised an untrusting daughter. Why do you think there's a trap behind every question?"

Evelyn didn't have the energy to answer that there generally was a trap behind each of her mother's questions. Her mother put a hand to her sternum.

"Everything alright?" Evelyn asked.

"Why wouldn't I be alright? It's just a bit of indigestion. I'm not used to this kind of food."

"Yes, mom. I know." Her mother had nearly gagged when presented with a corndog by the tiger enclosure.

"I only asked about school because Mia mentioned some bullies. Apparently, some young thug has been going around and setting fires."

For a moment, Evelyn wanted to see her mother's face when she learned that Mia had been in the principal's office three times in the last year. Evelyn was also called in to troubleshoot her daughter's fire-setting tendencies. The school encouraged her to discuss fire safety with Mia and sent them home with colouring books with pictures of fire hydrants and dogs in hats.

They walked around to the other side of the bear enclosure and saw that one was asleep at the top of a tree. There was no other movement. Mia cried and Evelyn thought about her white eyelashes. She pressed her hands against the glass and left a trace of her prints behind.

"Maybe one will be awake next time," Evelyn said to no one in particular because Mia was already running off to pick up bits of ice cream cone from the ground by a garbage can. Mia had to compete with a chickadee for the sugared pieces. If her grandmother weren't watching, Mia would have stuck them in her mouth just to see the disgust on Evelyn's face. Instead, she put them in the garbage bin and smiled at her grandmother. When her grandmother returned the smile and turned away, Mia wound her leg up behind her and kicked the chickadee. A feather floated down and landed beside Mia's laced-up shoe—Evelyn's mother brought a hand to her ribcage as though she wanted to push herself inward.

"Do you need to rest? You look a little pale."

"I'm fine," she said. "Stop pestering me."

Mia ran back to them.

"Are you going to die soon, grandma?"

There was a slight sheen across her grandmother's forehead. "If I can find a bench without chewed gum across the top I'll have a—"

"Mom, I really think you should sit down, you don't look good."

"I'm *fine*. I don't know why you're poking at—"

"Look," Mia cried, "a bear!"

Evelyn turned around knowing that there was a statue of a bear on the other side of the bush. Mia laughed and for a moment, Evelyn laughed with her. This was exactly what she would have done at Mia's age. Evelyn turned to her mother and smiled (some of the underlying tension had been released. Now they could go home and consider the day something of a success) but her mother's hand was on her throat hiding a sharp intake of breath she would never let go

You will remember something
about crumbs. Were you supposed to
leave breadcrumbs to find your way back?
Did you forget? Is that why you don't
know where you are? Is that why you feel
the burn of bread as it moves through you?

The school was an older building with a tatty Canadian flag blowing in the wind, a few kid-sized bikes chained to the stand which had probably been there since October, and a cup full of blood that had been overturned against a snowbank. When Evelyn got closer, she saw it was a red Slurpee. Evelyn held a coffee in each hand and then maneuvered the front door by holding one against her chest and hoping that the lid wouldn't pop off. Once she was through the door, she smelled shoes and furnace filters that were stretched beyond appropriate use. She didn't need to look at the arrows on the wall that would guide her towards the principal's office.

As she entered the main office, she tried to undo her scarf without putting down either of the cups. The heat was mounting as a particularly strong vent pushed air from above her head.

"Hello, I have an appointment with the principal."

"Ah, Mia's mother. Yes, we're expecting you. Please take a seat, she'll call you in a moment," Danny DeVito said.

Evelyn hadn't quite known what to expect. Would Mia be in this meeting? Was this a meeting just for the adults? There was a good chance Mia was still in her classroom, fingerpainting (or something equally useless) while Evelyn had to sit in the principal's office and receive a scolding on her daughter's behalf.

"Come on in," came a voice from the next room. "Make yourself comfortable." These last words were spoken before Evelyn had even set foot in the principal's office, like a script running a few lines too early. Evelyn wondered if they were directed at her or at whoever the victim directly before her happened to be.

"Mrs. Tate? You can come in now."

Evelyn held one half drunk Americano in one hand and a full cup with coffee stains dripping down the white sides in the other.

"For you," Evelyn said as she extended the cup as an offering.

"Thank you, Mrs. Tate. That's very… thoughtful of you."

"I know you must be busy."

"Yes, well. Let's discuss our situation with Mia."

"Yes," Evelyn said, "let's." They took their seats.

"You see, Mrs. Tate. The hair cutting is only the tip of the proverbial iceberg, as it were. We are actually far more concerned about some of Mia's other behaviour. She's always been rather quiet and very perceptive, but lately she has begun telling other children stories that parents are finding... troubling, let's say." A small bead of sweat dripped down the side of the principal's forehead and hit the desk with a sound louder than it had any right to be.

"What kinds of stories?"

"Mia told a number of students that she was a witch. She also said she had swallowed a snail and that it was feeding from her stomach lining. And that if other children bit their nails, the pieces of nail would embed into the sides of their intestines and eventually they would bleed out. And that the hair she collected was for a woman who lives inside the willow tree in your backyard." Evelyn felt a bead of her own sweat trailing down between her eyebrows.

"As you know," Evelyn began, "my mother died last year. She and Mia were very close."

"Yes, and I am so sorry for your loss." The principal straightened a bronze apple on her desk and turned it around so that Evelyn could see it was an award for administrative excellence. "However, Mia's behaviour is concerning and should be addressed sooner rather than later."

A brief flash of movement caught Evelyn's eye and she looked to the window behind the principal's desk to see a figure crossing the snow-covered field. There was something familiar about the halting movements, about the gait, about the slight drag of the foot.

"Mrs. Tate?"

"Yes, sorry. What do you suggest?"

"Counselling, perhaps. Generally, fantasies like these can be dealt with swiftly through counselling."

"Counselling. Okay, we'll try that."

The figure in the field took a few more steps until it stood next to a goalie post as though taking a moment to catch a breath.

"Would you excuse me?" Evelyn asked.

The principal appeared not to hear her. "We think it might be best if you let Mia stay at school for the rest of the day. We wouldn't want to interrupt her learning journey."

"No—we wouldn't want that."

Evelyn gathered her scarf, coat, and mittens and caught a hangnail on a loosened thread.

*You will walk and walk and walk
and walk. You do not know how to breathe
without your lungs. How to distribute your white
blood cells without your spleen. How to digest
the scone without your large intestine. They have
all been punctured and placed in a bag. The bag
is placed in your stomach. You will pause and wonder
what to do next. You will not know what to do next.
There is no other movement. Only you.*

She shook the principal's hand, (which was sweatier than Evelyn had expected) and retraced her steps to the car. Evelyn had already begun thinking through the logistics of driving her daughter home with the body in the back seat. Mia normally sat on the left, but she could probably be persuaded to sit on the right if Evelyn bribed her with ice cream. On second thought, Evelyn would not need to introduce Mia to the body—she would politely ask the body to leave the car before she went back to pick up Mia in the afternoon. Before she left the office, Evelyn had noticed that the principal hadn't taken a single sip of the Americano. It was sitting, precariously, on the edge of the desk as though the principal might accidentally knock it over and have an excuse not to drink it. On her way to the car, Evelyn could see that the figure in the field was gone.

The left-side passenger door gaped open and a small pile of scone crumbs covered the plastic mat on the floor of the car. A tiny bit of fluid pooled on the leather seat and there was an oily ghost of a handprint on the window.

You will step and step and step
and step until your feet should bleed
but there will be no blood left in your body.
You will lie down beneath an evergreen tree
and its needles and sap will break down
what remains of you until there is nothing left.
You will spill. You will feel a pull back
towards the earth. You will dribble.
You will—

Publication notes

"Twisted" was originally published in the *Minola Review* and was a finalist for their inaugural fiction contest judged by Heather O'Neill in 2020. "Nectar and Nickel" was published in *In/Words*. "Garden Bed" appeared in *Tap, Press, Read* published by Loft 112 and was featured in the Calgary Central Library short story dispenser. "Bruised Plums" was published in *The Town Crier* through *the Puritan*. "Red Strings" (originally titled "what we lost in the fire") was the second-place winner in the 2016 Blodwyn Memorial Prize for Fiction. "Home Burial" appeared in *Release Any Words Stuck Inside of You, an Untethered Collection of Shorts* published by Applebeard Editions. "Wisteria" was published in *Persephone's Daughters*. "Someone is Dead" is forthcoming in an edited anthology entitled *ReVisions: Speculating in Literature and Film in Canada*. Segments of "The Fridge Light" have appeared in *the Antigonish Review, Clockwise Cat, Canthius,* and as a limited-edition leaflet published by *the Blasted Tree Press*.

Acknowledgements

This collection would not have been possible without the support of some very special people.

My family: Greta LeBlanc, Gerry LeBlanc, Katie LeBlanc, and Aideen O'Toole.

My mentors: I am forever grateful for the support of Suzette Mayr, Larissa Lai, and Aritha van Herk. Each of you has taught me so much (most importantly, to believe in myself and my writing). I hope to make you proud.

My friends and colleagues: Adrienne Adams, Heather Adams, Heather Robertson, Rachel Shabalin, Dania Idriss, Ryanne Kap, Ben Berman Ghan, Ryan Stearne, Alycia Pirmohammad, Marc Lynch, Calum Robertson, Logan Pollon, Kyle Flemmer, Kat Heger, Leah and Sarah Van Dyk, Maryam Gowralli, Shuyin Yu, Allison Iriye, Samantha Purchase, Melody Dowdy, Jamie Michaels, and Xen Virtue. You are all wonderful, creative people and each of you has had a hand in this book in some unique way—thank you.

Thank you to the Great Plains team for making this book a reality!

Lastly, thank *you* for reading. Stay spooky!

Amy LeBlanc is a PhD student in English and creative writing at the University of Calgary. She is the author of the poetry collection, *I know something you don't know* and the novella, *Unlocking*. Her work has appeared or is forthcoming in *Room, Arc, CV2, Canadian Literature*, and the *Literary Review of Canada* among others. *Homebodies* is Amy's first short story collection.